ALL SAINTS' DAY

ALL SAINTS' DAY

Brent Benoit

Sewanee Writers' Series / The Overlook Press

First published in the United States in 2002 by
The Overlook Press, Peter Mayer Publishers, Inc.
Woodstock & New York

WOODSTOCK:
One Overlook Drive
Woodstock, NY 12498
www.overlookpress.com
[for individual orders, bulk and special sales, contact our Woodstock office]

NEW YORK:
141 Wooster Street
New York, NY 10012

The chapter "Concierge 1996" appeared in a somewhat different form
in the Fall 1999 volume of *The Greensboro Review*.

∞The paper used in this book meets requirements for paper
permanence as described in the ANSI Z39.48-1992 standard.

Library of Congress Cataloging-in-Publication Data

Benoit, Brent.
All Saints' Day / Brent Benoit.
p. cm. —
1. Accident victims—Family relationships—Fiction. 2. Children—Death—
Fiction. 3. Loss (Psychology)—Fiction. 4. Louisiana—Fiction. 5. Brothers—
Fiction. 6. Cajuns—Fiction. 7. Grief—Fiction. I. Title
PS3602.E666 A44 2002   813'.6—dc21   2002072465

Book design and type formatting by Bernard Schleifer
Printed in the United States of America
FIRST EDITION
ISBN 1-58567-312-9
9 8 7 6 5 4 3 2 1

For Duffy and Laura Mae Benoit
and Albert and Hilda Lissard

Acknowledgments

Thanks to Amy Williams at ICM for nurturing and finding the right home for this book. Thanks to Wyatt Prunty and the Sewanee Writers' Conference, and to Tracy Carns and David Mulrooney and The Overlook Press for publishing it.

I appreciate the guidance of my teachers, Moira Crone, and especially in my impressionable youth, Paul Kelly. Chase Adams, Greg Baxter, and Steve Stern offered encouragment in times of futility. Special thanks to Alison Lurie, Diane Johnson, and Tim O'Brien for saying something nice.

I appreciate and love my family Frank and Linda and my sister Michelle who listened and helped me. But most of all thanks to my life, Meredith and William Luc, who give me light and reason and worth.

ALL SAINTS' DAY

Vision's Son
1961

ULYSSE LAY FLAT OUT ACROSS THE front porch dreaming of horses. He was waiting for his father to take him to the Sunday race. His chest rose and fell in rhythm. The ankle bone and naked heel of his foot tapped the corrugated tin beneath the porch. The rubber toes of his tennis shoes pointed outward from kissing heels at the threshold of the door. One toe pointed east toward the oil field and the other west toward the long black asphalt road.

Dust powdered his eye bandage like beignet sugar. The bandage was tied with a bowknot around his head. He inhaled deeply once, like drinking the air, and held it. He listened for his mother's footfalls on the linoleum of the kitchen floor. There was nothing. He decided that she was very far or very close. He lifted the sides of the bandage with his thumbs. Light flanked his bruised eyes as if it had been an enemy lying in wait, but he kept the bandage raised, light straining his eyes, feeling like a heavy weight pulling him forward. Then it felt like water going into his head. He was swimming in it, his eyelids pinned back by the force of it.

"Arête ça, Ulysse." His mother's voice was high off. The sound became a bank he was trying to swim toward. "What, Momma?" he called to her.

Then he felt her hands on him. Her fingers smelled of raw meat and pepper and the same store-bought perfume that all the oil-field mothers wore called American Gal. It smelled cheap and obvious. He loved it and hated it both.

"Leave it on." The bandage was dry and flush against his face again.

"I wanna take it off."

"Listen to the TV. I'll put the long ranger at the window."

"It's the Lone Ranger. And I don't want it, Momma."

"You gonna be heavy-headed just like your father, you." He knew she meant to say thick skulled or pig-headed but didn't know the right English for it.

"Let me be, Momma."

"Go on by yourself. Daddy'll be home soon enough."

"Why's Daddy got to work on Sundays?" She did not answer. She was gone again.

Ulysse could feel the heat pressing down on him. The front of his body was simmering, but the back of him, which lay in direct contact with the porch, felt cool and dark. He heard a rustling in the dry grass and the slow wrenching grind of the trucks on Esther road.

Esther was the name of the dog that belonged to the regional director of the oil company. Mr. Donald Kipper of Houston, Texas. Every family member of Mr. Kipper had an oil-field road named for them. Sons, daughters, cousins. By the time the Maringouin oil field was cut, the Kippers had run out of relatives. So as a kind of joke they named the Maringouin oil-field road Esther Road after their dog. It was rotten. It wasn't right that the name of the street his home was on was the same as some man's dog in Houston.

His mother's singing fluttered through the open window. Her voice was slow, and the words of her songs were indeterminable. Not in French and not in English but two ribbons weaving one sound. Almost words and then only humming. Just the buried lyrics trying to rise and getting held back somewhere deep in her bird throat. The faucet water running flat and smooth against the bottom of the sink occasioned this. He could almost smell the okra in the sink, the green pellets and the aromatic membranes that now, he imagined, covered his mother's fingertips.

Ulysse could hear an approaching rustle in the weeds. It crunched beneath the footfalls. It was his father, Adam. Usually Ulysse went off to the neighbors at suppertime knowing his father would be home. During the day he would get anxious as the clocks thin arms traveled closer and closer to six o'clock. But lately he'd been fine. Ulysse had worn the bandage since Tuesday, and it made his father remember what he'd done to his son.

"What you say, Russell?"

"Nothing, Daddy."

"How's Momma treating you?"

"Just fine, Daddy."

Ulysse could feel his father standing beside him. He did not move, and the smell of him was strong of oil and cigarettes and sweat-stained khaki cloth tinged with the industrial soap Ulysse's mother used to wash their clothes. His father pulled the bandage back from Ulysse's eyes.

Ulysse's hair was cropped close to his head. His father had seen the Maringouin supervisor's boy from Beaumont come down in a Buick. The next day Ulysse's father had taken him to the barbershop and gotten him the same haircut.

"Hello to you, Daddy." His mother was at the front door.

"Hello, Momma," Adam replied. "Le diner est pare?"

"No. I got it cooking though."

He pointed down at the boy who had finally gone to the doctor when he admitted to his mother that his vision had been blurry the last few days.

"Did the doctor call with the price? Combien-ca coute?"

"Rien. Rien."

"Combien?"

"Thirty-seven dollars and twelve cents."

They were both quiet for a moment.

"Did he say anything else about it. Ask anything?"

"I told him he fell."

"Russell, you want to go for a ride?"

"No, Daddy. Don't take him. I got dinner on. And stop calling him Russell, Daddy."

"Nothing wrong with Russell. Russell's a good American name. Ulysse's too coony. He won't get nowhere with a coony name, Momma." Ulysse knew his father meant coonass, the name Texans and people from Shreveport and Baton Rouge loved to throw around.

"We'll eat when we get back, Momma. I want to take Russell for a ride."

"Not the races. Don't you take that boy to those races."

"It'll be good for him. What you say, Russell? You want to watch Cousin Gilbert race that horse I told you about?" Adam was rubbing Ulysse's head. The boy didn't answer, unsure of how things would go.

Then finally, "Yes, sir."

"You didn't do it, Adam. Tell me you didn't do it."

Ulysse heard his father's boots plunking against the hollow plank floor. He could almost see the dark air beneath the house vibrating with Adam's steps. It made him shudder. Then he shut the door, slamming it hard.

"Why you . . . why you buy that thing? You bought a horse? That was our savings, Adam. That was the money my momma left me, Adam." She was pleading her case but could not go on, for tears ruined her speech.

"I told you. Don't question me on this. Don't question me. I only got half of the horse, and Gilbert got the other. There's some money left."

"How much?"

"A week's worth to get by on."

She didn't call him names but just started crying, knowing not to argue. This didn't make him aggressive but instead made him plead with her.

"You'll see, Babe. You'll see. We gonna treat that horse like a prince. Gonna race him just right and build a real racer with him. We gonna feed him honey, and he's gonna sleep in bed with Gilbert." He paused at this fishhook, waiting to see if she would bite, waiting for a smile. But he went on, so Ulysse knew she hadn't smiled or laughed silently or anything. She was upset for sure.

"It's an investment, you know? An investment. What you wanna be? Like this forever? Living with all these other coonasses in this hole? Eh? No. I'm gonna build something with that horse, something for all of us, yeah. Comprende? Slowly and slowly we gonna build all our money up with the horse until we can leave the oil field. You see? It's just gonna take a little patience is all. And some faith in God, you see. I see God in that horse, Babe. He is like lightning in a horse. He's the whole dang Bible in muscle and bone and leg, you see?"

From the porch Ulysse could smell the okra burning in the pot.

"But the glasses for him, Adam. The glasses," she said, her voice weakening at the thought of the glasses.

"Babe, I'm gonna take care of that. I'll get it today. I promise on my momma's grave, Babe."

"All that money. What are we gonna do? Leave him

on the porch till he learns to cane chairs, Adam? He's gotta go back to school, you know."

This upset Ulysse. He saw himself at twenty, his eyes white as eggs as he sat weaving rocking chairs for tourists from out of state. They'd take pictures of him and tell people at home how they met an authentic blind Cajun in Lou-z-anna.

"No. It's gonna be just fine. That horse is gonna save us, Babe. He's gonna be like Jesus. Like Jesus' horse, Babe. Come on."

"You blaspheme, you," she said like a mother chastising, but with no teeth to the criticism.

"Come on, Babe." He was holding her and forcing his look into her eyes, forcing her to look at his eyes and swallow the lie and laugh with him at his Jesus' horse joke. And she did, slapping at his shoulders playfully. Ulysse could hear it through the thin door, and hearing it brought it to sight in his head well enough. He had seen it too many times not to know what it looked like now.

Something was rattling in the truck, but Ulysse couldn't tell what it was. The windows were down, and he could hear the country, the absolute silence of the fields beyond the engine. When the truck stopped, Adam told Ulysse to sit still until he returned. Ulysse sat alone in the truck but he could not decide where his father had stopped. He pulled the bandage up from the bridge of his nose. The light bled bleary and violent into his eyes. Lines and shapes swooned before him. The same thing had happened once last week while he was walking back from the oil refinery where he had taken his father some coffee. The telephone poles on the road had all bent toward the horizon. The sky turned up, puckering from the refinery to the fields beyond the asphalt road. Ulysse had stumbled to the tarmac and rolled down into a ditch. He waited there for Christ to appear riding a white mare from on high, like Silver from *The Lone Ranger*. He listened with his eyes shut for the sound of the trumpets. Nothing came but a splitting pain in his head and nausea that took hold of him completely.

Now the light parted away. The roadside was empty. He looked off beyond the truck. The tin roof of a house turned upward at the sides of its gable into the shape of a cradle. Then two figures appeared in the doorway of the house. The door was crooked. It warped in a fit of dark empty space like a wavering black flame out of which two figures emerged. It was his father, red skinned, and his Uncle Gilbert, a small man of five-foot-three.

He saw how dark his father's skin was compared to his uncle's. His father was half Indian. His mother's parents had forbidden her to marry his father because Adam was too dark with his black hair and brown skin. So they eloped. Ulysse was dark too and the kids at school had sometimes called him *t'negr*. He hadn't known what to say. Once there was a boy who came to school and spoke no English, only French. The boy was small, sparrowlike. He tried to open the windows on the bus saying "fresh, fresh." Ulysse called him a coonass and punched him.

The other boys never called him *t'negr* again. Ulysse's stomach sank every time he thought of that.

Gilbert wore a jockey shirt, red satin. It was untucked and fell over his khakis. Ulysse could see them, and his eyes went into another fit. The men's bodies twisted like roman candy in the now blue light of the day. He felt a terrible spasm begin and he covered his eyes again.

"Commen' ça-va, Ulysse?"

"Bon."

"Don't speak French to him. I don't want him to be an ignorant like you and me."

"Easy, Adam. You listen to those Texans too much."

"I'll bust you open, Gil. I swear I will."

"Settle down. We gonna race that horse or beat each other up?"

Ulysse could hear his uncle's voice brittle and high. His father's voice was low and steady. And then they were in the truck. The two men spoke in French to each other at first. Ulysse could understand only a few words like *horses* and *son of a bitch* and *money*. He understood *d'argent* for money. His father would not allow Ulysse to speak French in the house. But his mother and father often spoke it when they visited with family or if they were talking about something they did not want Ulysse or his older brother Pavil to understand.

Ulysse listened closely. He heard the word for *money* again and for *doctor* and then what sounded like *blue glasses*. Then Ulysse knew what the men were talking about. The doctor had told his mother that he needed tinted lenses to correct the damage done to the inside of his eyes.

"Where you gonna get that kind of money at?"

"I'm looking at it."

"Don't put me there."

Then they began to speak in French again, and this time Ulysse could not understand them at all.

The racetrack was four miles down a single thread of gravel road which almost reached the town of Ramah. His father called out.

"Well looky here. I never seen so many fancy cars in one spot."

The cars lined the plank rails of the track. There was always a gathering of workers' trucks at the gates and another gathering at the finish line. Elsewhere they were far apart. The rails of the track bowed downward under their own weight. Beneath the two-by-eight wooden rails, wider planks had been driven into the ground with hand mauls and these were buttressed intermittently with random lengths of two-by-sixes. The tracks formed two separate lanes inside of which two horses ran to one line. These horse races were not legally sanctioned by the parish, so they had always taken place in the backcountry, past the highway and the rice fields.

It was the same track that Ulysse would come back to as a man. Standing alone in the mud at the center railing which had been replaced by metal poles. Walking from the gates to the finish line, watching the horses bolt from the gates and expecting that feeling to spark inside him. He would stand at the railing, clutching the metal. Looking and looking. Anxious for some feeling to come up in him each time the gates opened.

"Who's all that?" Gilbert asked, gesturing at ten or so new clean cars parked on the far side of the track.

"That's what Arceneaux did. He told Richards and Fleming and Jussen and all them higher-ups at the refinery."

"All them are here?"

"I figure so."

Ulysse could smell the cigarette smoke now. The tobacco smelled fine along with the worn-out fake leather smell of the bench seat.

"Are you riding Vision's Son?"

"I got him in the stalls out back. Why? What you thinking?"

"They got a horse?"

"Richards had one. Supposed to race him at two o'clock."

"Two?" Adam looked down at the watch hanging from his belt. It read a quarter to one. "You better go on then."

They walked in single file toward the stalls on the north side of the track. The supervisors' cars were parked crooked and shiny, the bulbous hoods, glaring of wax. The only dust on the fenders and hoods was the soft and finely pounded dust of the quarter-mile track. "Put your hand on the rails," he said, reaching Ulysse's hand to the rough-cut lumber of the stalls.

"Hey, boys," a voice called out. Ulysse heard a man talking fast and high directly in front of them.

"Mr. Matthews. Hello, sir." Gilbert said.

"Hello, boys. What you old boys got going here?"

"Just a little racing, sir."

The man looked around at the track and the horses in the gates.

"It's fine. Yes, fine," Mr. Matthews said.

Ulysse lifted the bandage until he could make out the man's face. It was clean and smooth and shiny. His hair was dark and wet-looking and combed back, parted with one straight line down the side. He looked like the pencil-drawn men in the Brooks Brothers ads in the New Orleans Sunday paper. Ulysse had never seen such a person, and it was strange, like a visiting dignitary from a faraway place, which must be the place movies are made and magazines are photographed.

"That your boy, Bueche?"

"Yes, sir," Adam replied.

"What's wrong with him?"

Ulysse cut his shoulders back. He wanted to step behind his father, but he knew he shouldn't.

"He fell off the porch. Sleepwalking."

"No kidding. That's too bad."

"Does he talk?"

"Sure. Say something, Russell."

"What's up, Doc?" he said like the cartoon and felt a soft palm on his head. An awkward silence fell. Ulysse could feel them looking at him. They looked at him the way grown-ups, particularly men, will look at a boy, sizing him up for manhood. He felt them trying to decide if he would be worth anything.

"Hey, son. Is your name Russell as well? That's my boy's name. That's swell."

When Ulysse didn't answer, the man shifted his attention. "Are you a jockey, Gil?"

"Yes, Mr. Matthews."

"How bout that. You riding that chestnut stump over there?"

The men were silent again as if looking where the man had directed.

"Yes, sir. They're bringing him in the holding stables now. That's Vision's Son, my quarter horse."

"Vision's Son? Is he fast?"

"Fast as hell."

"Good. Mr. Arceneaux told me about you people's little race here. I think it's charming, really neat. He paired my horse with yours for the two o'clock. I'm taking two of my horses to Alabama to stud. Got them in the trailer."

"You running them both, Mr. Matthews?"

"No. Just the young one. I'll play with him. The other is too well bred for the likes of you all. Wouldn't want to rip up his legs on this old dirt track. My boy, Russell, will ride him. Russell's a helluva rider."

Suddenly from behind the men came an explosion of sound. The starting gates ripped open. The synchronized springs gave. And then the voices of the men on either side of the track started to yell. Wild and guttural voices.

"Allon! Allon! Go you couyon, you!"

The shouts rose from the men standing on car bumpers and flatbeds. The thunderous cadence of the horses' hooves beat against the soft dirt of the track. Then the voices sank away, and the sound of the horses was gone as well.

Inside the stables the stalls were small as coffins. But they were dark and Ulysse could pull up the bandage and rest it upon the clipped hair above his forehead. His Uncle Gilbert stood at the back of the room, one leg raised up along the rough-cut steps that led to the ramps. Gilbert tucked the frayed bottoms of his khaki trousers into his worn-down leather boots. When he stood up from the ramp, Ulysse could see that he now looked like a jockey.

The horse watched them from the back of its stall, almost suspiciously. Its eyes were dark and glossy in the low light that shone from a single bulb hanging in the center of the room.

"You get the papers from Bruck like we talked?" Adam asked.

"Put money down to Mr. Bruck. He's a fine horse. He's Vision's offering."

"I know what he is. Did you get the papers on him? He looks like that horse Paratonnere."

"No."

"Then how you know it's legitimate?"

"I get the papers on final payment."

"You're a fool, Gilbert. That horse is no more Vision's offering than I am."

They all looked at the horse.

"Sure he is. It's the horse you and I went and looked at."

"Maybe so. Johnny been fixing him?"

"No. He's clean. Never had a shot, not once."

"Get Johnny down here. Russell, you stay with Uncle Gilbert till the race. I'm going to make a bet."

And then his father was gone. A blur of rectangular light shot into the room from the open door and then it was dark again.

"Ulysse, va cherché ca cable."

"Ehh?"

"Hand me that rope."

Ulysse walked to the wall. A long stiff rope was fastened to a nail. He pulled it down and brought it to his uncle.

"You don't speak French no more, Ulysse?"

"No, sir."

"Why not, Ulysse?'

"Daddy said there ain't no future in it." He watched his uncle fasten a belt around his gaunt hips. "Daddy said the only place I am allowed to speak it is the graveyard. Cause the graveyard is the only place where French is gonna be spoke in this country. By the dead ones, I guess. Cause I guess if you wanna talk to Maw Maw Bueche and Paw Paw Bueche they won't understand English no how."

"Your daddy is crazy, Ulysse. Nobody cares one way or the other bout those things but your daddy. It don't make you more successful or a better person. It just makes you less than whatever you already are to act like you're not what you are. That's how I see it anyhow."

Ulysse could see his uncle's red satin shirt in crimson flashes. He saw the horse. Its head was drawn down to the rails, but suddenly it looked up as a man pushed aside a loose wall board and sidled through.

The man handed a syringe to Ulysse's uncle, and his uncle handed the man a palmful of folded bills.

"You can pet on him, son," his uncle said after the man went back out through the loose board.

Ulysse ran his stubby fingers along the horse's nose, feeling the bones beneath its hide. What did the horse's skull look like, he wondered. The horse's hair was dark and fine like Ulysse's hair. He stroked it and it felt like his own.

"You like that horse?"

"I love it. I'd want to be a horse."

"What you mean? You mean you want to be a jockey?"

"No. I mean a horse. I'd like to be one."

"That's fool talk. Nobody can be a horse."

Adam came into the room. Sunlight flooded the doorframe. The room blackened when the door banged shut.

"I set my money on you."

"How much?"

"Don't worry about it."

"Not too much, Adam?"

"Don't worry about it. Where is Johnny? He gonna fix that horse?"

"I don't want to fix him. I never raced him here before."

"You get Johnny and you fix that horse. Or I'll fix him myself."

"You better not. You'll kill him if you give him too much."

Cursing quietly Gilbert slammed out the door. Ulysse stood small in the corner. He watched his father pacing back and forth just beyond the perimeter of the electric bulb's light. His father mumbled to himself, numbers and words in French. He was a blurry dark figure by the door. His cigarette glowed tiny and red like a fire viewed from a great distance.

Ulysse stood by the horse. The horse moved back in the stall as if it were trying to blend into the wall. It stood unmoving at the very rear. His Uncle Gilbert came back in.

"Well?"

"Johnny's not around," Gilbert said.

"What you mean?"

"He's not anywhere," Gilbert said.

"Well, you got to give it the shot."

"I'm riding it. I can't give it no shot."

"Come on. There's not a thing to it. The needle's on the table?"

"I reckon so."

"We'll wait till the gates," Adam said. "That's when Johnny does it. I seen him."

It was five till two by Adam's watch when they finally got Vision's Son to the starting gates. They led the horse straight up the scuffed metal ramp and through the rusted rails to the gates. Ulysse had covered his eyes again since the sun was bright and high and hot in the sky. He allowed himself to see through a small slit in the bandage. His father walked closer to the starting gates. Gilbert sat atop Vision's Son in the pen.

Before they left the stable, Ulysse had watched his father take up the syringe and insert it into a small clear bottle. The liquid went up into the syringe until the bottle was empty. Adam rolled down his khaki sleeve, covering the syringe with his cuff. He took Ulysse's hand and walked out to the starting gates while Gilbert rode the horse.

One man stood on top of an old Ford. He held a green towel in his left hand. When he began to speak, the men on either side of the track turned to face him. The men turned away from their pads and pencils and their dollar bills and faced the man on the truck. When he spoke, men at the center of the clusters of other men made a cutting motion with their hands at their throats to say that no more bets would be taken.

"We got two good horses today. Over here is Mr. Matthews's brown horse called Checkers. He's a fine horse out of Kentucky and on his way to Alabama to stud.

And over here in the south track we got Gilbert Bueche's horse out of Lake Charles and is a direct descendent of the multiple winning racehorse Vision."

The men on both sides of the track laughed uproariously.

"I'm the pope's bastard, *me*, if that's Vision's blood," one man called.

"Gentlemen, no more bets. The names have been called."

Ulysse could not see everything that he wanted to see from the space between the rails. But he found his father's hip by his left hand. Looking at his father's waist, he saw the watch hanging there. Two o'clock. He saw his father's hands move toward the broad red hindquarters of the horse. The thin sliver of the needle. A vein compacted into squiggles and winding around the horse's muscles. To Ulysse it looked like the Himalayan mountain range as it appeared on the globe at school.

The needle found this mountain range, the raised and distinct blood vessel. The horse went into convulsions, rapid and violent. The man on the truck raised the green towel above his head. Ulysse walked to the front of the horse. Its eyes were shocked and bulging as if Ulysse was a walking fire approaching him.

The horse struck like a snake at Ulysse's hand which rested on the middle rail. Then the gates sprung open. The sound was sudden and stupefying. Ulysse did nothing but stand in place. The horse shot into the dirt and the sky. Ulysse looked down where the horse had bitten. A chunk of rotted wood the size of his fist lay on the ground. The edges of it were wet.

With the gates torn back furiously by the springs, the sun poured in bright and bleary. Ulysse watched the track. A dust trail billowed up behind the mass of the horses churning straight ahead. Then his head began to ache.

The track rails bent out toward the north, turning in a crescent across the horizon. He watched the lines of the track for them to bend straight again but the track went further out in a warped and buckled line. The men and the cars they stood upon turned into the warping rails. The rails were crooked lines as if they were turning on a carousel around the racetrack. Ulysse sat down in the dirt, his head swirling. The voices of the men were somewhere on the periphery, someplace that was distant and irrelevant.

When he woke, it was dark and cold. He felt the rough-cut timber of the barn table against his back. He was in the stalls again. He must have been carried there. A few men stood on the railing and leaned over it, looking down into the stall. Two voices stood out above the others. When one man would say his part, the other would respond and then again back and forth to each other. Waking up during this conversation made it seem that all there had ever been and all there would ever be were the two voices blurting back and forth in the dark room.

"I won't do it."

"You must."

"I won't."

"He is going to anyway. Too much in him. Look at that leg anyhow."

"You then, Gilbert. It's your property too. You do it. Take my pistol and do it."

"No, Mr. Matthews. I can't."

"You people are something else."

Ulysse could not see the figures clearly where they stood just beyond the light of the bulb. They darkened and faded when he looked at them. Slowly he began to make out a red silk shirt. And then a khaki shirt and heads atop these forms. He could see another head like an older version of his own. And beside that he could see a dark blue jacket and a red knotted tie and dark wet-looking hair and a mean silver snub of a pistol, pointing at darkness below the men's knees.

"Go on then, Bueche. For this much. Take this and do it. There's more there than you'll see in a month at the oil field."

Before Ulysse closed his eyes again and before the loud echoing, before the ringing in his ears and the report which felt like a tender fleshy bell exploding in his head, there was only the sound of breathing. He could not be sure if it was his own breathing. Loud and low. Terrified and weary. What had at first seemed like his breath, his noise, had moved away and entered the horse that struggled against the darkness below the men. Breathing, labored and thankful against the stale wet dirt.

The next week, Russell's mother took him to the drugstore in Maringouin. They ordered the prescription glasses with the money his father had received. They went to the drugstore two weeks later, and when he walked out wearing the new tinny frame spectacles, the street was straight and his mother's face did not melt when he looked at her. Everything was shaded blue like the haze that comes on before a rain. Lee Street seemed to have frozen over since he last saw it. The egrets were tinted blue like life had gone out of them. Lights on the pharmacy sign and the people walking the sidewalks looked frozen in skirts and suits of blue. Even his mother's face was colorless and dull.

They lived in the Maringouin oil field long after most of the other fathers had moved or been promoted to Texas. When Russell turned eighteen he had raised enough money working in the new plant for a car and could go away. He stayed away for a few years. But like everybody said, only those who turned millionaire or queer left Maringouin for good. And sure enough after a while he came back.

Girl on a Bicycle
1968

I T HAD BEEN TWO NIGHTS SINCE DOREEN HAD slept without waking up, her hair tangled across her face and the sensation of radiation coursing through her body like invisible drilling particles. The nightmare was always the same. First she felt every atom in her composition infected. Then the room about her was charred black. Rising from her bed she walked down the smoldering hall. The charred skeletons of her mother and father lay beneath the sheet of their bed, and when she pulled it away, their bodies turned to ash, crumbling like the pages of a burned book.

She woke everytime from this nightmare to the pale yellow walls of her room and the bluish tint of morning hazy over the fields behind the house as the cattle congregated at the barn, come in from wandering the dark fields, ready to be fed by her father. She thought of her parents.

"How can they sleep?" she wondered. "How can they?"

She knew that they would all die in the night. At thirteen she had not lived one day without dreading nuclear Armageddon. It delivered a surreal plasticity to her life and all the people and things in it. Each person lived as if the bombs weren't pointed at them, as if there wasn't a gun aimed at the head of America. Everything was a play to Doreen, a pretension that life would not soon cease, as she knew it most certainly would. And in this sense the world to her, which was Maringouin, was not shaped and formed by the unchangeable past but by the irreversible future, all things becoming inverted and measured from markers not reached as opposed to before she was born when time was measured by markers gone by. All life was already filled with ghosts—ghost dogs, ghost girls and boys, ghost policemen, ghost pigs, and ghost pigeons—whose hour of death was certain but unknown.

"What will happen to us?" she asked her mother.

"Honey, I've told you this already. The Lord won't let us die. He will come down and take all of us away."

"How will he know who to take and who not?"

"He will take the ones who have accepted him into their hearts. The ones who believe he has died for our sins."

"What if he makes a mistake and forgets someone?"

"He won't honey. He won't.

At first these words comforted Doreen. Poor saps,

she thought as she rode her bicycle past the block of Vietnamese shrimpers who occupied the slanted tin-roof houses between the railroad tracks and the infinite cane fields. Poor people. She had walked at dusk by their open doors and seen plank rooms flickering in candlelight across the bellies of Buddha statues and smelled the clean gulf odor of boiled shrimp and steamed rice. But then she wondered, where was it recorded that she had been saved? Had she really accepted Jesus into her heart as her mother had? What if she only thought that she had accepted him and she really didn't do it one hundred percent. What then? Would her family leave her to be tattooed with a 666 on her forehead as they ascended with new clean wings above the cane fields and smoke stacks of the sugar mills and oil refineries?

She rode her red Schwinn bicycle down Lee Street. The deeply muddy bayou was wavering beside her. Shrimpers trolled slowly up to the fish market while men with wide-brimmed hats shading their faces smoked hand-rolled cigarettes in a put-put bateau, its cypress hull covered in empty crawfish nets and gill seines as they navigated toward the Atchafalaya.

The ground flared in straight lines beneath her, creating a sense of fantastic speed. In her wire basket lay a bag with sandwiches, and a thermos of coffee for her father, and her transistor radio. It was Saturday, but her father, who worked at the sugar mill as a mechanic, had been hired along with many other men to help dismantle and number framing members, beams, whole dormers, sections of porches from the old plantation house on the bayou. The plantation house was one of the oldest houses in the parish.

She peddled up to the antebellum mansion. The fantastic dormers that had once sat atop the sloping hip roof lay in the front yard beside the row of oak trees that had been planted in 1830 and once lead carriages and now cars toward the porte cochere beside the house. Her father was pointing at a section of the house which had been painted with black numbers. A tremendous section of cypress shutters was labeled Sa-Sww for detachment and eventual reattachment after the house was relocated. He smiled and removed his cap when she came up. The sun lit his bald head.

"Hey, cher baby. What you bring Daddy?" he asked her.

She told him she had sandwiches and coffee. So they sat down beneath one of the monstrous oak trees and ate together. Occasionally Acadian men or black men would walk up to her father and ask him questions about the dismantling of the house. He would answer them, and they would shuffle off quickly, saying, "Ah. Ah. Okay." Some of the men spoke only French, and her father would talk to them in French. They all seemed to respect him very much, which made Doreen feel that she too was important.

"Why are you tearing down that house, Daddy?"

"To move it. Somebody wants that it be done."

"Is it true what everybody says about it?"

"What you mean, cher?"

"Some of the kids said it was wrong for them to come and take the house, Daddy."

"It's just a house, baby."

Some of the townspeople in Maringouin did not want the house torn down and taken away. But a man from New Jersey had driven by the house on a trip to inspect one of the oil refineries. The man had seen the old plantation house slumping in the yard at the end of the oak alley and decided to buy it. The man was interviewed in the *Maringouin Morningstar*. He had stated that his daughter was a tremendous fan of the book *Gone with the Wind* and that he was transporting the house piecemeal to one of their properties in New Jersey or Connecticut where it would be reconstructed for his daughter's birthday.

But on that summer Saturday, as Doreen sat beneath the shade of the oak on the cusp of time, with the demolition of the entire planet more likely than the slow unfolding of life, her father asked her what she would do with the day.

"I'm going to ride my bike out on the bayou road."

"Don't go by yourself, baby. It's not safe for a little girl to ride by herself in the country."

"I'll be all right, Dad. I'm fourteen."

"You're only thirteen, baby."

"I know, but almost."

"Just don't go too far. Not too far, all right, baby?"

The dust made a rising trail in the air as her tires rolled across the dirt road. Doreen watched a crow's black wings fan the sky. She stopped to pee behind some bushes. She took the transistor radio out of the basket of her bicycle and flipped the switch. The country air was filled with the voice of Bob Dylan vibrating coarsely over the road's washboard ruts. She decided to ride as far as she could or until she got halfway to darkness at which time she would turn around, since she had no lamp.

Cattle on the other side of a barbwire fence turned their woozy heads toward her and straightened their huge spines, emitting deep guttural calls which Doreen imagined welled up from the blackness of their many stomachs. She would occasionally see a water moccasin slither over the road toward the water. The further Doreen rode away from town, the older and more sophisticated she felt. And then the town did not exist for her. She could no longer see it, and she realized she had left it on her own for the first time in her life. She felt herself expand beyond her own limitations of self-image, beyond the daughter, the sister, the eighth-grade student. She was an explorer, an adventurer. With no one from town to see her and label her, she was free. She removed her hands from the handlebars. The red plastic tassels whipped like banners in salutation and celebration of the moment. She craned her head toward the sky and pedaled blindly.

Suddenly the front wheel of her bicycle hit a rut, and she fell to the thick grass beside the road. In that instant she felt that the violent jerking plunge was God's way of putting her in her place. With blood and grime caked on her knee, she sat in a daze and began to shake, but she did not cry. She wet her thumb and wiped away the line of blood on her shin. Picking the bike up, she saw that the chain had gone slack.

"Shit," she said.

The sun was directly overhead, and the dust caught a breeze, gathering on her pedal pushers. She flipped the bike over and began to fit the chain back onto the sprocket.

A car approached, a black Cadillac. Reflected in its hood was a black world—black road, black sky, black trees. The silver grille blazed with elongated sun sparkle. A fantastic coiling wake of dust billowed like tawny clouds, ripples that morphed in the townward breeze. Doreen could see figures inside the car. At first they were like the shadows of people, geometric and slim, that architects drew in renderings of proposed structures—ghosts of the future who haunt the clean lines of buildings yet to be built.

Slowly standing she began to make out the faces of people. A woman had cheekbones that made Doreen think of doves. A cylinder hat concealed her hair, and sunglasses in the shape of black plastic hearts covered her eyes. She was smoking a cigarette. With the woman looking at her Doreen felt as if she were a little girl with a bicycle in the country and nothing more. Other people in the car. Men, another woman perhaps. A flash of dark blazer lapels, thin matching ties, and fists languidly gripping the steering wheel, and then the car was gone, leaving nothing but dust so that she couldn't see or breathe.

When the dust settled back down to the road, Doreen turned the bike over and began riding along the bayou once more. She rode like this, hands firmly planted on the bars, viewing the land—all fields of cane or cattle with an occasional oil derrick or cluster of old-growth trees bordered by rusty ribbons of barbwire fence.

Then she saw the dual monolithic columns of red brick where a new clean pea-gravel road commenced. This was the Matthews place. It had to be. The dirt road continued, but weeds and grass became dense and there were no more ruts in which to ride.

Everyone knew about the Matthews place. Mr. Matthews of Hoboken, New Jersey, had built it in six months flat. It was said to be the most modern house in the entire state of Louisiana. People said that all houses would one day be like the Matthewses' house, all glass and rich dark wood in box shapes. Dishwashing machines, air-conditioning, garage doors that opened automatically. And televisions. Four televisions, they said. One was in a bathroom and one was supposedly on a patio. Rumor said that Mr. Matthews also had an underground lair with concrete walls two feet thick. The children of the men who'd built the house talked of a subterranean paradise. False windows in the concrete walls looked out on photographic murals of mountains and oceans backlit by fluorescent lights. A year's supply of canned foods. A deep water well that trickled in the central room across a concrete fountain.

Doreen was slack jawed with this thought. Standing

with her bicycle between her legs, feet in the clean pea gravel, she stared up the driveway that cut through deep pinewoods when an explosion shook the ground. She felt it beneath the rubber soles of her shoes. It rattled the sky. Sound attacked every cell inside her—more than mere sound. Sound did not grab you and pummel you.

"Atom bomb. It's the atom bomb." Doreen thought. Her stomach fell—like on the Ferris wheel at the parish fair. She saw her family in sentimental freezes: her mother looking down at her from the kitchen sink, her father squatting beside the house eating pecans and gazing at the fields, her brother playing sheriff in the yard. They were all dead. They were all smoke. She knew it. And she was riding her bicycle up the gravel drive toward the house of Mr. Matthews. Some automatic mechanism which clicked into gear was navigating her toward the house. What luck that she should be here when it went off. No. It was predestined.

Then she remembered the angels coming for the saved ones. Had they taken her family? Did God know about that one secret, that one shameful thing she'd done to herself in the bathtub? That was it. That was why she'd been left behind. It wasn't her fault. How could she tell Father Carvel about that? Her mind went on like this, her concentration turned inward so much that she didn't look up to see the black Cadillac racing toward her. But the blaring horn bore down on her, the grill all shiny and chrome. She jerked the handlebars left, missing a bulbous headlamp by mere inches. Looking over her shoulder she saw the smoke, billowing black smoke ascending toward the clean cloudless sky. The atom bomb had struck town. Maringouin was burning.

The Cadillac stopped and a head popped out a back window. It was the woman. But she wasn't wearing the hat or the glasses now.

"Are you all right?" she yelled.

Doreen nodded.

"Are you certain?"

Doreen continued nodding her head dumbly.

"We've got to go, young lady. Are you certain you're all right? All right then. You mustn't be here. This is private property, little girl. Will you go back to the road?"

She nodded again. Then the car sped away. She thought a moment later as she continued toward the house that they must have believed her to be mute.

The house was fantastic. It had more glass than all the stores in town had. Solid oak beams spanned the width of its flat roof, and its windows reflected the surrounding woods in clear resolution. People must have been wrong about the mushroom cloud part, she thought, looking through a gap in the trees at the sky above town. It wasn't a mushroom cloud at all but a black column of regular old petroleum smoke.

The ornate oak door stood slightly ajar, so that she could see a long white smear of sun glaring across the parquet floor of the entryway. A bronze knocker hung in the center of the door, but she ignored it and slipped in. A man paced back and forth. He would stop to smoke his cigarette and look out the massive wall-length windows, then start pacing again. Doreen could make out the stylish cut of his brown suit, the black phone in his left hand, and the cigarette clenched in his fingers as he swatted the air.

"How many, Phil? . . . What d'you mean you don't know? . . . Find out damn it! Go on."

Hearing her or sensing her, he turned abruptly and faced her. His face and hands, shrouded in gray smoke, shone pale amid his dark hair and dusky clothing.

Doreen spoke. "Can I get in your bomb shelter, Mr. Matthews?"

He put his hand over the mouthpiece. "What are you doing? You can't be in here. Get out!"

"I won't be trouble. I can . . . I can do things . . ." What could she do? She could twirl a baton. Before her eyes there ascended an image of herself as a twenty-year-old woman in a ragged sequined outfit twirling her baton before the cigarette smoking Mr. Matthews.

"Phil!" He turned toward the windows and the woods beyond as if Phil were outside the glass. "Well, how many? . . . At least five? How many are missing? . . . Oh. My God. Who are they? I mean, were they? . . . No white hats? . . . Good. That's something anyway. I'm coming down. Monty said I should be there for the papers. It will look best that way . . . No, don't try to tell me that! I've already sent Angie and my son and the others to the airport. They'd only been here a day."

He hung up and took a last drag of his cigarette before flicking it angrily at the big windows.

"Did the bomb go off, Mr. Matthews?"

He turned and looked at her as if he'd forgotten she was there. "What? No. No bomb. There was an— You're dad doesn't work for me does he?"

"Yes, sir. He's working on the Boucodray house, taking it apart for you."

"Oh. But not at the refinery right, sweetie? Your daddy doesn't work at the plant, does he?"

She shook her head.

"Well, there's been an explosion at the plant on the other side of town. Some damn valve ignited. I'm not sure. I've got to go there. You've got to leave, little girl." He picked up his keys and a briefcase marked ACCOUNTS.

"Come on. I'll give you a lift."

"I have my bike." She looked back at the open door behind her.

"It'll fit in my trunk."

They drove along the silent road toward the smoke which had formed a tarry ceiling above them. It spread out over the fields. Mr. Matthews was a fidgety driver. He smoked and mumbled to himself. Doreen figured him for forty or forty-five, about her father's age, but somehow he still had an air of youthfulness. Perhaps this came from his adolescent haircut or his broad jutting chin or the way his thin red tie hung slack below the oxford collar around his tendony neck.

As the red convertible—with the top up—glided toward town Doreen watched the towering oil derricks that appeared periodically in abandoned pastures. The sign in front of some of these rigs read MATTHEWS OIL & GAS EXPLORATION CO. She looked back from the signs to him and wanted to say, "That's you." It excited her.

"Do you have a wife?"

"What?" he said, giving her a perplexed look. "Yes, of course I do. She was just here. Just came down. And then this happened. Those idiots. I can't leave for one damn hour before they blow the place up."

"I thought an atom bomb went off."

"Oh, that's silly. That's all you kids think about nowadays."

"I know. I just thought it was though."

They drove along quietly. He kept smoking. She watched him. She knew her thoughts did not coincide with how she looked to him. She knew one day her body would grow into the domain of her thoughts about men. It was like a seed sprouting in her head that only she could feel and know. But for now she was just a girl to him.

"I have a daughter your age."

"You do?" she said as if she didn't know.

"Sure. She's the cat's whiskers, my little girl. I'd do anything for her. She looks just like her mother, you know."

Doreen thought about this. She thought about the house.

"Sweetheart, you wouldn't repeat anything you heard me say on the phone back there at my house would you?"

Doreen didn't know what he was talking about. Had he said something she shouldn't have heard?

"Never," she said.

He looked relieved. "It's just that sometimes we hear things we shouldn't, and we must respect the person who—I mean—" He broke off, not smoking nor mumbling, just watching the road.

He stopped the car on Lee Street at the grocery store. He removed her bicycle from the trunk.

"Thank you," she said. He bent to set the bike down. Cautiously Doreen raised herself on tiptoes and kissed Mr. Matthews on the cheek. But he didn't seem to notice. The sky was filled with smoke, and flames sprang above the trees beyond the town.

As Mr. Matthews drove away she got on her bicycle and headed home. Traffic clogged the outgoing road. People looked frantic in their cars, holding cloths or just hands over their mouths and noses and over the faces of their children. Doreen rode faster and reached the plantation house. People down the street were running and jumping in cars, honking and screeching off.

Doreen knew her father would be at the house, and she decided to wait for him. She stood beneath the oak tree and looked at the house. Her eyes followed the scrolling millwork of the porch and the violin shape of the dormers resting on the ground. The air stung more and more as she breathed it, and she became very tired. So she lay down among the bony roots of the tree, and the house seemed to sway in the wavy light. Her mind tingled and she closed her eyes.

An hour or more passed before she woke up to an

alien face peering down at her. Goggle eyes and a leather apparatus with small holes in its strange mouth like the spout holes in her mother's watering can. She realized it was a gas mask, and a man was carrying her. He placed her on a white cot in the back of a van with white walls. He put the mask on her and closed the double doors. A siren shrieked scary and watery above her as she fell back to sleep.

Doreen followed the story of the plantation house for years to come. And other plant explosions occurred in those years too. But none swept such poisonous fumes upon the town as that one had. A year or two later she read a magazine article with photographs of the house, which had been repainted a ferocious yellow and rested among a grove of snow-drenched pines in Maine or Minnesota.

She often drove by the fantastic dueling rows of oaks leading to where the house had once been, and she waited for the day to tell her children about it and to describe it to them in every detail.

A few years later one of the new casinos on the coast came and removed all forty of the ancient oak trees and planted them in front of a high-rise hotel. Most of them did not survive the transfer, but eight or ten confused-looking trees grew crooked and mangled in front of the asphalt parking lots of the Biloxi casino. So years later, when Doreen began to tell her children about the old plantation house as they drove by the place it had been, no house and no oak alley remained, only a field of weeds and empty oil barrels. But she would tell them about the house and her father and Mr. Matthews and the plant explosion. Later she saw in a national magazine that the house itself had been turned into a type of second-rate theme park called Dixieland! in Minnesota by a Greek immigrant entrepreneur. The plantation house served as the park entrance where people bought tickets and popcorn. The park had a few good years in the 1970s and then decayed into failure and bankruptcy.

The Matthews house at the end of the Bayou road suffered a similar fate of abandon and was eventually put on the market in the eighties but no one could afford it. It became the shell of a house where wind blew hard through its broken windows and hollow rooms.

Linoleum 1972

THE SHED WHERE THE WASHING MACHINE and dryer and iron were kept sat away from the house. It was a wood-slat barn with oily tools—ballpeen hammers and coffee cans full of greasy bolts—stored on the shelves. Under the light of a single bare bulb, Doreen pressed the suits for her mother, as she had promised she would do. She worked until the lapels and creases were crisp against the ironing board. When she was done, she thought about it. All during the ironing she had not thought about it.

The porch light flicked on and she composed herself, walking to the house with the two wool suits. Hooking the wire hangers on her fingers, she opened the porch door and stepped inside the kitchen. Her mother sat hunched like a scarecrow taken down from its pole.

"Let me see," she said.

Doreen held them up and her mother brushed over the plastic, examining the blue suits, one larger and one smaller but otherwise identical, purchased at Sears and Roebuck in Lafayette should they ever be needed.

"Good girl. Make sure your Daddy and Ellis don't wrinkle them up when it comes time to wear them. Somebody's gotta take care of it. And I can't trust either one of them to do it. Your father means well but he's simple. And Ellis, that couyon, him."

Doreen tried to laugh but couldn't.

"Listen," her mother told her. "Listen. I'm gonna stay with you," she said in the blessed space between coughing fits. A tissue was wadded in a ball on her knee at the edge of her gown. But Doreen wasn't listening, couldn't listen. "Take Jesus down."

Doreen looked at the lithograph portrait that had been scotch taped to the false grain of the cabinets above the stove since she was a girl. She carefully pulled it loose. She had never held it in her hands, but now she did and could see the smile on his face. Jesus looked silly staring off out of the frame, like he was posing for his senior portrait.

She handed the picture to her mother, who tapped the portrait as she spoke. The kitchen table was empty. The table was never empty except after the men had gone to bed. No saucers, spoons, cups, plates. Not the bottles or the angular elbows of her father and brother and her father's friends drinking coffee cup after cup and smoking cigarettes.

"I will go, but Jesus will be with you, Doreen. He'll

be with you. All that I am is him. You see? That's all I am. Like a container of him. All that has ever loved you was him loving you. Do you believe, baby?"

She nodded, wanting to speak, but too afraid she wouldn't be able to control her voice.

"You always been my good girl. Always."

Doreen wanted to tell her mother that it would be all right, that they were taking her into the hospital just to be safe and that she would get better there. There would be no need for the blue suits. Doreen wanted to burn those damned suits. She wanted to comfort her mother. But all those words had drained out of her so that all she could do was listen and watch her mother's face, wondering what it would look like in the coffin. She was unable to think of anything else.

"You gonna be fine, Momma. I know it."

"Take care of your daddy, Doreen. And Ellis too. Let Him do it for you," she tapped the lithograph again.

"You better get some rest, Momma. We got a big day tomorrow."

"You right, my baby. Such a pretty girl. Let Momma stroke your hair."

Doreen knelt on the linoleum floor and rested her head in her mother's lap. Her mother's small cold hands stroked the hair behind her ear. It was the last night they spent together in the kitchen.

Number 3
1973

WHEN I WAS FOURTEEN MY BREASTS came to me. They didn't sneak into the bed overnight. It was like getting fat or being pregnant—the way you change shape slowly and don't realize it. You feel just like yourself, like you were wearing a mask that no one noticed. It is when someone notices, when someone says, "Hey, you're getting fat," or after they pass you in the grocery aisle you hear, "She's really starting to show." That's when you feel like a different person. It was the same way with my breasts.

When I was a kid, I went every Thursday to pick up meat from the butcher at Cazayoux's Grocery on Third Street. I rode my bicycle down the Grosse Tete Bayou Road, turned on Lee, leaned my bicycle beneath the awning over the loading dock, and entered the shop. With a dollar seventy-five my Momma trusted me to buy the best deals that Mr. Cazayoux would afford our family. Buying quantities of beef for a family of four people, three dogs, and two cats, meant mostly beef heart, tongues, and poor cuts of meat like chewy sirloins and fatty ribs. My mother would start the roux at seven in the morning though, and boil the celery, green onions, garlic, and cayenne pepper until I got home at four-thirty with the meat which was immediately dropped into the pot.

Mr. Cazayoux looked like a walking piece of meat, red-skinned with pepper grime in the crevices of his ox neck. He had always been sweet to me as a little girl, taking his blood-stained paper cap into his hands, crinkling his brow with the utmost sincerity as the widow's peak of his forehead dipped almost between his eyes. He looked like the pictures of Huey Long that I'd seen in the school hallways. Robust and boisterous.

"You sure are looking pretty today, Miss Doreen."

He called me Miss even though I was only a kid.

"Thank you, Mr. Cazayoux."

"You want to look at our specials today? What is your momma wanting?"

"She wants pork roast if there is any."

"Oh no. None in quantity for less than two dollars."

He sat down on the bent-legged cane chair by the butcher's block, the legs bowing outward from his weight. He lit a cigarette and checked the doors twice with his eyes.

"Tell you what, sweetheart. I'll give you four fillets for two dollars."

"All I have is the one seventy-five, Mr. Cazayoux."

"Guess you'll have to give old Mr. Cazayoux a hug to make up the difference."

I didn't hesitate to hug Mr. Cazayoux. He was one of the nicest adults I knew. But when I fit myself inside his arms, he clenched them all the way around my back. Knocked the air out of me for a second. Then I felt his fat fingers squeezing my new breasts. He had wrapped his arms all the way around me and then some.

"My, somebody is growing up."

I froze like some insect paralyzed by the venom of a spider. When he let go, disappearing to the front of the store, I stood trying to decide what had happened. He dumped the wrapped fillets in the wicker basket attached to my handlebars and told me to tell my father hello.

It wasn't until later when I spent the night at Trilly's house in town that I understood. We were talking about boys and if anyone had touched us yet or kissed us. I told her about Mr. Cazayoux. She explained to me that he was feeling me up, that he was probably a pervert. I nodded like I knew this much already.

"That's what fillets are, stupid. They're titties you eat. He was probably feeling you by the pound." She roared in that convulsive laughter of hers and kicked at the pink wallpaper flowers. "Doreen got to second base with the butcher!" I had to laugh.

Trilly was on the softball team with me all through high school. She was good and went on to play in college. Nobody thought Trilly would make it to college softball. Everybody was sure I was going to be the star pitcher of the women's softball leagues, but they were wrong. All of them. Because everything changed four years later when I met Russell.

And where will you be now, Russell? You'll leave me and the boys too this time. Nothing but those damned checks with your scrawled signature on them. Like you were drunk when you signed them. Like you had to get drunk just to sign them over to me and send them in the mail. What if it comes back? What if my breasts were not enough? Will you take care of me again how you did the first time? Spooning soup for me in the guestroom in the front of the house. Covering me with your body when the fevers came. Telling me I was beautiful in that stupid wig. Why does it have to be hard all the time. Why can't we just be with each other? Am I not the wife I should be? Am I not the woman you need now, Russell? You're not a bad person, Russell. You just don't know how to be good. Maybe I should be able to show you. Are you afraid you'll mess up your own boys like your daddy messed you up? Busting us up. Busting us up. We never had a chance, you and me.

Sometimes I watched myself on the eight-millimeter films that Coach Patterson gave me. I'd project them on the white walls of the kitchen on nights before my treatment when I couldn't sleep. The little projector burned yellow images in a dinner-plate size on the wall. The purple and white uniforms were a blur. Elastic pants with stripes running from hip to knee. The older the film got, the more yellow the world that it projected became.

When I took the pitcher's mound, the players would emerge from the dugouts to watch, clapping in unison for the batter. The home crowd cheered my name in that chant: *Hot boudin! Cold couscous! Come on Gidot! Swoosh! Swoosh! Swoosh!*

My jersey fit tight then. Coach Patterson kept hassling me, but I wouldn't trade my small jersey with number 3 on it for a larger one with any other number. I even had a reputation for boys coming to watch me pitch in my jersey, or that's what Russell said. He told me later how his brother Pavil made him first come to a softball game to see me in my tight jersey. He said some of the boys came to the games only to watch me, which I knew was probably hooey. But I like the thought of it now, thinking about how I looked then.

Kneeling on the kitchen floor, I watched the film. I followed the path my arm took before releasing the ball. My left leg moved out first, forward and straight like the step of a soldier. My arm locked, my fist cupping the ball, my fingertips gripping the stitching—I drew perfect circles in the hot June night air. I felt the eyes of the crowd, the players, and the lights of LaFont Field all bearing down on me, as clay dust floated to my shins. Cicadas blurted in long walls of sound, and the batters' eyes were almost always looking off, too high or too low, sometimes closed, and the ball streaked past their bodies, rotating like a little planet that I controlled.

Jolly Adams, the sportswriter for the *Maringouin Morningstar*, said I was "unprecedented in the short history of women's softball." I pitched six no-hitters in the final two months of the season—seventy-plus-miles-per-hour pitches.

After the district finals I started seeing Russell. He would wait with Pavil by our team bus, sitting on that '68 Mustang, drinking Schlitz and crushing the cans beneath the heels of their worn alligator-skin boots. He walked up to me as I stepped onto the bus. He had a row of peach fuzz from ear to ear, and his blue-tinted glasses made his eyes as yellow as a cat's.

"Hey," I said, the last to board the bus.

"You're really something, out there," he said. "You from Maringouin?"

"I play for Maringouin High, don't I?"

"Sure. I'm from there too. I work in New Orleans now though. We should go out sometime."

I went to the back of the bus. White rectangles of parking lot light tumbled down into rhombuses and triangles on the seats. The Mustang fired, revved, mufflerless. "Free Bird" blared across the lot. His car roared in circles around the bus, fishtailing almost into the galvanized steel light poles of the parking lot. Russell emerged from the passenger window, sitting on the door, one hand gripping inside the door and the other one high above his head as the car sped around the bus, screeching and sending up the smell of burning rubber and exhaust.

The other girls pressed up against the windows of the bus, palms against the glass, gazing at the spinning Mustang. I did not fight for viewing space but closed my eyes and listened.

"I love you, Number 3!"

It was the voice of that scraggly boy with the tinted glasses. Was it some kind of joke? I thought maybe partly it was and partly it wasn't. The girls chattered curiously as the Mustang peeled out toward the new clean concrete of the interstate. I sat alone, closed my eyes, and put my hand to my chest. My whole body hummed electric, like the transformer in our backyard. If someone had touched me at that moment, that's how I would have felt to her. I whispered his name, my head bent down on the back of the seat in front of me. "Russell. Russell. Russell."

The next game we played Roseville High, and it rained in the fourth inning. After everyone had gone, Russell stood at the corner of the parking lot. White light patterned the hood of his car as I walked toward him. The passenger door was open. Daisies lay limp and damaged on the bucket seat.

We dated, spending every free afternoon together. It was too soon. He was twenty-one years old. I was eighteen. My mother had died that April, and besides Trilly no one had held me tight since she passed away. I put all that out of my mind, and Daddy hated me for it. Ellis hated me for it. But it was going to be a fling. He took me to highway lounges where we'd laugh and horse around. Daddy wouldn't let him come into the front yard. If only he had liked him, sometimes I wondered how it would be different. Russell was leaving for a three-month tour on an oil cruiser. In three months I would be at USL with Trilly, reunited to conquer the college softball leagues.

That summer was the state tournament finals in New Orleans. I had a scratchy game, but we beat Rummel High 7 to 3. Photographers from the school and the newspapers at home and in Lafayette rushed around us. Then there was a trophy in my hands, and the other girls lifted me onto the shoulders of the team. We took pictures for an hour. Pictures of the whole team with the trophy. Pictures of individual players with awards. Russell hadn't come out on the field but stood at the edge of the bullpen watching us, watching me and grinning. I stayed behind as usual, talking to Jolly. And when he left, only Russell and I remained in the middle of the field, atop the red dirt of the mound. We walked across the field, under the bleachers, and out behind them.

He pulled at my wrist and the MVP plaque fell to the concrete. He kissed me and held me, his arms wrapped so far around me that his hands almost came around to my breasts. I stopped him.

"Why?"

"Just don't do it like that, okay?"

"All right," he said, his voice only a whisper. He gently pinned me against one of the pylons beneath the bleachers. I could see my name carved into the brass plate of the trophy plaque: DOREEN GIDOT MVP—1973. My mouth went soft and wet as the stubble on his chin chaffed me. I wanted to speak, to direct him, but there was no voice in me. All my thoughts turned to ice in my skull, and I could not draw them out. He lifted me onto his hips and pulled open my jersey, working off the athletic bra with his hands.

"You're so beautiful," he said.

I felt his hands beneath me, the air damp and cool on my hips. Grasping the small of his back I pulled him to me. The line of the bleachers and the floodlights above drew distinct lines of shadow and white light on the ground, where half-eaten corndogs, cigarette butts, beer cans, coke bottles lay scattered across the concrete foundation. I couldn't believe how much filth there was.

The railing was cold and sharp against my back as Russell thrust inside me. I could see my most valuable player plaque lying amid the litter. And I suddenly wanted him off me. I wanted to get to the party with the other girls. I wanted to feel the plaque in my hands, the wood and brass, and to read my name on it and think about what that meant.

Then the sound of circuit breakers being shut off echoed across the field, and darkness came in quadrants. Right field went dark, then center, then left. Then the parking lot lights went off, and all I could see were Russell's eyes. His glasses had fallen to the ground. His eyes did not meet mine. I could feel his hand cupping me, then his face across my sternum.

"My legs are about to shake right off," he said.

We were married in the fall when the leaves left the trees bare, and the days were short. Whitaker came in December. My Merry Christmas baby.

Angel Boy
1978

I SAW YOU DIE, ANGEL BOY. IN THE YARD behind the house. Doves cooed in the woods. My angel brother. Momma calls you her angel son and Dad does too. We ask you to watch over us like you have super-powers, and ask for you to be watched over in heaven too. We make it sound like you got the good deal, Angel Boy.

You did not even have a nickname yet. Not Ferd nor Ferdy. But still the hard and shiny leather of a name. Ferdinand. Ferdinand Adam Bueche. I was Whitaker Bueche, and my brother was Clayton Bueche, and Dad was Russell Bueche—had been Ulysse but now was Russell—and Mom was Doreen Gidot Bueche. And you were Ferdinand Adam Bueche like our grandfather Adam Bueche who you must know by now.

I thought I should explain things to you, because I

don't think anybody ever did or could have. So I sit here in this room in this city, and my voice echoes between the high ceiling and the plank floor, and I stare at the perfect blue wavering flame of the space heater. I sit in this dark room and smell the clean flame and watch the tiny fantastic shadows dance across the metal wall of the heater, and I talk to you.

Violet sleeps beside me, her hair dangling down off the bed, and the blue flame makes a soft glow across her naked back and stops at the canal along her spine.

I will explain things to you and hope that you can hear me. They just took you and put you away and nobody thought about explaining to you because there is no way of doing that. So you have to be quiet and not get told anything forever, and people go to see your grave and cry for you, but they don't tell you anything. But you must promise to leave Clayton alone, Angel Boy. You must whisper it to me in my dreams.

You must whisper: *I will leave poor Clayton alone.* And you must go to Clayton and tell him: *I forgive you for killing me, Clayton.* You must issue it. You must pronounce it with your cherubic voice which came to you there and not here. A voice without confusion or doubt, God-lit and innocent. That's what you are, Angel Boy.

Do I remember it? Oh yes. I remember the sky glazed blue. I remember the green lawn sloping to the river where you fell. I remember watching television in the living room and Momma going back and forth to the toilet vomiting. She'd begun her fight with the radiation machine. Her brown hair collected in the corners of the rooms. Sometimes I would go to her kneeling on the tiles of the bathroom floor and pat her on the shoulder.

Death was hunkered in the shadows of the bathroom, kicking her in the belly, yanking the hair from her skull, playing dirty how death does. And trying to make her look just like him, bone thin and unspeakable, the way you are now, Angel Boy. She would spit into the toilet: *You're not taking me. I'm not going. You took my angel son, my Ferdinand, and you are going to have to fight me. You took my momma too, stole her from me. You can forget it, son of a bitch.* This was the only time I ever heard her cuss. Four in the morning, while everyone else slept. She would not lie down in the stupor of the bed. She would not fall to the mat, would not let it be a fixed fight.

Death didn't take you like that, Angel Boy. Sometimes I picture death crouched skeletal in the trees smoking a corncob pipe, eyes glowing like coals. Then it pulls up its monk's robe, darts through the trees, and jumps the fence like a track star leaping a hurdle. I dream of it grabbing you with bony claws. Then it clears the opposite fence and bounds into the woods.

The day you left us, they all argued about who was supposed to be watching the twins. Clayton and you were only fourteen months old and Uncle Pavil and Dad both were there. *Slow down, boys! Slow down!* Dad hollered. But you didn't notice or know, giddy with your new legs. Whirling and bumping into everything, panting and going at it again.

By whoever's design it was, you were quicker than

Clayton. You had been walking for a long two months, and little Clayton could still only shuffle around on hands and knees, crawling like an animal crippled on the highway. He would scrape at the ground, trying to catch you. But you were a teaser, Angel Boy. Anytime people would visit, they'd see you on your straight white legs, trotting from room to room like a little boxer, and they'd see Clayton struggling to catch up to you. Inside his knees would be caked with lint and fur from the dog, and outside there were grass stains on his little blue trousers.

People would say, "That one is a whip," meaning you, Angel Boy. "Yes he is. And handsome too. Look at those brown curls and those green eyes."

"The other one is a little slow looks like."

Once someone said, "Funny how it happens like that. Born at the same time but so different."

It didn't help Clayton that you were talking too, that you could say words like *tree* and *shoe* and *cat* and *dog* while Clayton was still moaning and babbling. When you'd say *shoe* or *doo-doo* or something, Clayton would unleash a mess of sound. People's heads would turn at the monstrosities Clayton would sound out, angry verbalizations of wanting to say something. For all they knew, Clayton was the future town loony.

Nobody could blame Uncle Pavil for not expecting what Clayton did. Who could have known that your twin brother, who looked nothing like you, would stand up in the yard that fateful day and do what he did? It was completely unforeseeable.

I was standing on the porch looking down to the yard. Uncle Pavil sat in an aluminum lawn chair beneath the fig tree. He was smoking his Camels. He always smoked by the fig tree, so the August preserves seemed to taste of nicotine—syrup and broken figs spread on his morning toast. You were over by the pier, Angel Boy, just looking toward the water and pointing and saying, "Water, Water."

Uncle Pavil sighed smoke at the tree and said, "That's right son. That's water. What a whip. He's a whip all right."

Clayton crouched on the lawn. He strained and suddenly came up on his feet, standing unsupported for the first time. Then he took a step and, like a gambler who knows no better and bets again, took another step. Uncle Pavil hollered up to the house for them to look out the windows.

No sooner did Uncle Pavil yell and Mom and Dad rush onto the porch, than Clayton staggered toward you and fell against you. And with the sickening sound of your head hitting the concrete pad before the pier, you did not rise again. When we got to you, you sort of smiled.

Dad wrapped you in a blanket and did not wait for the ambulance. We went in the station wagon. I remember looking out the back window and seeing Uncle Pavil in the driveway. One of his flip-flops had fallen off, and he was holding Clayton cockeyed in his arms as we drove away. Momma held you in her lap. Your eyes gazed at the ceiling of the car, and your mouth was set in a little O like you had seen something, a face or maybe a picture that you recognized.

Then everything was long and cold and white, with a clinical smell just like you would expect. They told me to kiss you, so I did, and your forehead was already cold. When I close my eyes now, your eyelids are a red bloom and your lips blue. Sometimes I'd go to Grace Church and put a note in the glass vase by your grave asking you to watch over me, because Momma said we knew a friend in heaven who could take care of us. But later when I'd go back on my bicycle and check, the note was wet from rain, and the words had bled.

All Saints' Day
1979

WITH THE WINDOW ROLLED DOWN, even with the radio on I could hear their voices outside the car. It was a long time ago, when Dad worked at the Texaco plant. I was almost seven. Clayton was two. Ferdinand had been gone for only a year.

"Don't go to Grace, Doreen."

"Why don't you come?" my mother asked. "Whitty, roll that window up before your brother catches his death."

Dad watched the pavement, disconnected. In the dim light of morning the blue lenses of his glasses made his eyes look as if they had been drawn and poorly erased.

"Why you gonna do this now on my last day at the plant? You promised you wouldn't, Doreen. Think I want it like this? Think I want to be away like that? It's for them I'm doing it, for you and Whitty and Clayton. We been through this. It's the only way."

"We are going to see him today. It's All Saints' Day. You should come."

"I can't. It's too hard for me. I've got to put in one more day. One last good day here. Don't you want me to be a good father and work my hardest?"

"Why are you leaving for so long? Why not come with us? So that we can at least be a family on this last day. You'll be gone so long on that boat." She fretted with her nail-bitten fingers at her mouth, her forehead furrowed as if she just realized he was leaving.

He turned to the plant, smoke rising from the concrete stacks. "If I come with you will you promise you won't want to go to Grace? Will you promise me that?" He took hold of her. "If you promise me we can go to the country. Take a boat even, on the river. Promise me you won't want to go there, and I'll stay with you. We'll go out and have a nice time. We'll have sandwiches."

"I can't do that," she said. "Not today."

"Well, I can't go and sit there and look down at him. I won't do it. I don't know how I'd keep it together."

"Going away won't keep us together," she said.

"Not us, Doreen. It's me I can't even keep together. Me. You better not go to the cemetery by yourself. You know that place is dangerous. Don't you take the boys there." He tried to stroke her hair but did it awkwardly. "Doreen, promise me."

She nodded.

The sun had still not fully risen. As I rolled up the window, the chemical plant sign shimmered in the distance: TEXACO. The word was at the center of something that everything else spun around. Texaco meant the place Dad was after we dropped him off on the slick asphalt in the morning. Texaco was where he was when the sun went down and we turned into the parking lot to pick him up again.

Clayton sat chattering in the station wagon's front seat. His fat chin quivered. I wanted to pinch it. Wanting to pinch Clayton turned into wanting to squeeze his fat face until he cried. I ground my teeth, pinching myself instead until wanting to hurt him passed away.

Outside Dad looked as he did when he cussed, his eyes narrowed, his face scrunched. I heard only murmurs, like a television with the volume down. Behind me, caustic music rose from the speakers.

With my finger I traced small holes burned in the seat. My mom would pick Dad up from the Lucky Stop on Highway 190, and he would pass out in the backseat, his cigarette burning beside his face. My pinky finger jutted into one of the holes, into the yellow foam beneath the plastic layer. There were two holes beside that one, and the three holes made a face.

The station wagon door whined open, and Momma got in the car, slamming the door hard enough to rock the car. "Busting us up," she whispered. "Busting us up."

Men walked toward the TEXACO sign. Beyond was a jumble of pipes: exhaust lines, fume lines, silver and tar covered. Yellow lights perched at measured distances up the smoke stacks. The plant glowed, each section of industrial white pipe reflecting yellow so that an electric aura crowned the entire plant. At the apex of the towering stacks blue lights flashed on and off inside the foggy cloud of exhaust. The pipes exhaled and the blue lights flashed making the smoke look like synchronized thunderheads. A chain-link fence ran around it all. It was scary and beautiful.

Dad went in at the gate. The word TEXACO ran from shoulder to shoulder in blocky red letters of a machine-stitched patch. Like all the other men who walked beside him. I felt better watching him shrink into the lights of the workhouse. I felt the same calm as when wanting to pinch Clayton left me. Momma was crying again.

"Is Daddy gone now?"

"No, baby. He's not leaving till tomorrow morning." She turned to me. "It's gonna be all right, Whitty." As she steered the car out of the lot, music lifted out of the speakers. I could hear her crying beneath Glen Campbell's "Rhinestone Cowboy" until I fell asleep.

When I woke, sunlight ached my head, and darkness behind my eyes throbbed. Everything beyond the window was moving. Thick brush rolled along in intricate variations, turning and flaring, swirling by on a long page. Birds were dried specks of black going straight across the clouds.

"Did you draw this for me?"

I looked up. Clayton's eyes were fixed on her, vigilant that she stayed close to him.

"Did you, Whitty? Did you draw this for me?"

I nodded, still sleepy. She was holding up a torn and smudged drawing that I had done in Mrs. Plitt's first-grade class. Waiting for the bus at the back of the classroom, I drew it for her.

"I think you are very talented, Whitty. What are you going to do with it?"

"I'm gonna give it to Ferdinand. It's a picture for him too."

"That's nice. That's real nice, son."

She smiled, her green eyes darting, her short black hair bobbing at her shoulders. The drawing rode the blast of heat from the front vents. Glided down to the cold seat beside me. Was it good? It wasn't anything like how I wanted it to look. Such things never seemed to match the vision in my head. That was always the most disappointing part of drawing. But my hands were pudgy paws when they held the crayons.

Spiderman rode the back of a bald eagle. I wanted the eagle to be noble and strong, like the eagle on the pinnacle of the flagpole in the corner of the classroom. But on the page was a red blob with white eyes globed over the inevitable V–shaped bird whose arched nose looked like Toucan Sam's. The talons were not powerful and victorious but red Cs dangling from sticklike feet. I dropped the page to the floorboard.

"Are we really going, Momma?"

"To the cemetery? Sure we are." She leaned over to my brother and dabbed with a wet thumb at the corner of his mouth.

"Why?"

"Today we are going to clean the graves where our family is buried."

"Why?"

"That's what we do on All Saints' Day. We clean the graves of our loved ones and make them shiny and bright. When I was your age, my momma took me to do it at this very place."

"At Grace Cathedral? When you were seven?"

"Yes. Right here at Grace Cathedral. And now we're the ones who do it."

"Daddy said we aren't allowed there anymore."

"That's not true. Grace is a safe place. Nothing bad happens there. But we're not going to tell Daddy that we went though, okay?"

"Why?"

"It's just going to be our special day. Just Mommy and her Whitty."

"And Clayton too, huh Momma?"

"Yep, and Clayton too."

On the floor opposite my seat was a purple bucket with rags and brushes. My father had talked badly of Our Lady of Grace Cathedral after he read in the newspaper that homeless people had taken up shelter there. The parish police had arrested drug users at Grace as well. There had been a photograph in the paper. A black police officer holding a hypodermic needle with plastic tongs. The officer looked alien, standing in a riot mask with tongs for hands.

"Are you mad at Daddy?"

She waited so long to answer that we came up to the big bridge where the Mississippi River opened vast and wide beneath us. Barges like iron teeth lined the banks. The green and rusty girders of the bridge zigzagged past. My hands sweated from the height.

Uncle Pavil had told me that some catfish in the river had grown bigger than him. They were blind and fat and strong as horses, navigating like muscles through the boiling currents. They never saw any light. I thought about that when we crossed the river—caravans of catfish nosing their way in the rushing water. Uncle Pavil got wound up about the catfish. "Think about how that must be, Whitty," he said, "to have to fight the river all the time."

"Why can't they rest?"

"They aren't made for rest. If they come up too high their brains might explode."

"Not even up by the bank where the water goes slow?"

"No, not ever. They have to stay down there in the mud and feel the whole river rushing over their brains. They have to fight the water all the time or else they wind up in the Gulf, in the salt and dead. And it's always dark for them cause they're blind. Their eyes are black as buckshot and just as useless. You have to be pure muscle to live like that, Whitty. Always hard and always dark."

"No," Momma said at last. "Daddy and me are fine, honey. Don't you worry about Daddy and me."

I knew better than to push it. You get an understanding of such things before you can even talk much. I looked at Clayton. He looked stupid. Oblivious. I wanted to pinch him again, so I bit my lip and looked out the window. The rain began.

"This is where you were born, stupid. On this bridge," I said to my brother.

Momma swung over the seatback and slapped my leg. "Whitty, don't talk like that to him."

But what I said was true. Angel Boy never got old enough to know it. Mom had come undone with him and Clayton as she lay in the backseat, with Dad driving like crazy into the city, trying to cross the bridge but stuck in a jam of cars. I was sitting beside him, and Aunt Irene was in the back catching Mom's babies. Clayton came out on the bridge, and Angel Boy came a little later but still on the bridge, so they weren't from any city or parish but were born in the air, suspended above the cold river that ran dark and sparkled like a swath of outer space.

The cemetery lay all around the old Catholic church, the one where everyone went before Immaculate Conception. It had been gutted by fire in the 1960s.

Mom steered the car into the parking lot, where we ate cheeseburgers and waited for the rain to end. The stained-glass windows of the church had been shattered by the heat, and the entire vaulted ceiling lay in rubble. The inner walls, exposed to the sky, were blackened in long sooty licks. The pews were heaps of charred wood.

Yellow laminated posters, tacked on large sheets of plywood over all the doors, said, ABANDONED! DO NOT ENTER. TRESPASSERS WILL BE PROSECUTED.

Inside the station wagon, Mom fed Clayton strained peas with a plastic spoon. "Eat now, my baby," she said, wiping his chin, and I squinted out at the rain, looking for Ferdinand's headstone.

Momma was sick from the time I'd been born. The cancer had taken both her breasts, and rampaged into her lymph nodes. It wasn't unexpected—not where we lived, next to the chemical plants and refineries in what they call Cancer Alley. At least one person in every family there had cancer or had just died from it. Cancer had taken Mom's mom already, and she said it had come for her too. But she wasn't going anywhere with it.

She had almost died when I was two. Dad would take me to the hospital to visit. I don't remember playing on the cold geometric tiles of the floor or the flowers drooping by the narrow window. I saw pictures later. She had told him to take photographs, so I would know I'd been there.

I remember hiding beneath Mom and Dad's bed in our house though. I must have been four years old. The carpet was brown and shaggy with bits of lint in the fray, and the bed linen's shadow made a line across the floor. I was not supposed to be in the room. When I crawled out from under the bed Mom was standing naked in the bathroom doorway. Her thighs were white with blue veins like tiny rivers coursing under her skin. Her belly was lit in a sliver of light. A moon belly with a flesh button where her navel had risen. That was the first time I saw the twins, even if they were behind the wall of her belly. Above it her chest was flat and close where her breasts had been removed. Scars ran parallel with her sternum like zippers. When she saw me she ran into the bathroom to cover up.

"What happened to you, Momma?"

She sat on the floor beside me, her face bland as a cup of milk.

"Remember when Mommy told you how sick she was?"

I nodded.

"This is where the sickness was. The doctor had to cut it out."

She explained it to me, how her mother had died of it, and asked if I understood. I didn't. She explained until I said that I did. And she let me touch the scars. My hand in hers, my fingers ran along the small ridges where the stitches had pierced her skin. She smiled, and I calmly pulled my hand away as if everything was okay. But I couldn't sleep that night. I paced back and forth in the hallway. Coming to the bedroom door, turning the knob silently. Opening the door, I entered the hot dark room.

"Can I sleep in here?" The hallway light cast a rectangle onto the bedroom floor. There was no answer. I decided to watch television until morning came. There were cartoons I liked, one with a black cat and a yellow dog. But they were speaking in Spanish, and I walked back down the hallway to her room.

"Can I sleep with you?"

"Not tonight, Whitty," Dad said. "Go back to your room."

The hallway was big and empty as a church. I didn't want to say it again, but I couldn't control myself.

"I told you already, you want a whippin?" Dad came into the hall, his hair twisted about on his head, his gold chain with a cross draped over his shoulder, and dragged me outside. Music played loud next door where my Uncle Ellis lived, and adults were standing around talking and drinking beer. When my feet hit the cold grass, I tried to run toward the crowd.

Dad grabbed my arm with one hand and jerked my pajamas down with the other. The people in my uncle's yard watched my father wallop my bare bottom with his open hand. They smoked their cigarettes and laughed. I hated them and knew they were not anything like me and that I would never be like them or my father.

Momma came outside. She called Dad a son of a bitch and pushed him so that he dropped me on the grass. His hands were by his sides as she pushed and pushed on him. The people stopped laughing. I ran across the yard toward the bushes at the back wall of the house and hid there. The sky was black, and the full moon grinned down on the yard.

When Dad found me in the bushes he held me and cried and said he was sorry.

"I'm sorry, son. Please forgive me. I promised myself I'd never be like that. I promised myself." It was good when he cried and held me. He never laid into me too hard or beat me for no reason. All in all he was a good dad. His tears and regrets and apologies made everything square, but still I didn't want to be around him. He made me uneasy. That's just how it is for some dads and their boys—if they are even good enough to stay on at all. Dads come around and sons' stomachs start to hurt, it doesn't matter why. That's just how it is.

So there I was in the station wagon with Mom and Clayton, and Dad was leaving again. I wondered if he would come back this time. I wondered what it would be like if he never came back and somehow Spiderman became my father. But I knew that was not real to think about. The sky was still low and gray, but the rain had stopped. Mom turned around to me, my brother pulled close to her chest.

"Grab the bucket, Whitty. It stopped raining."

* * *

From the station wagon window, Doreen studied the church parking lot. The pavement was splitting apart with weeds forcing their way through, slowly turning the unused expanse back into the field that once had been there.

"Everything busts up sooner or later," Doreen whispered. "Everything busts up."

She spooned strained peas into Clayton's mouth. Whitaker sat in the backseat eating his cheeseburger and staring at the burnt-out shell of the cathedral. Someone had spray painted on the walls. *Led Zeppelin*, a lightning bolt, *Smoke Grass*, a Confederate flag in blue with eleven stars, *Jesus Saves*, and *Maringouin Sucks It*. She was thankful that there was nothing too depraved, something Whitaker might ask about, but he didn't seem to notice.

As Doreen stepped from the car the sun came back out. She lifted Clayton to her hip. She held him more than she had held Whitaker. Maybe because she couldn't breast-feed Clayton. Maybe holding him so much made up for it.

She stepped down the old brick walkway that led to the iron gates. The walkway had overgrown with weeds. Scattered in the grass were slivers and shards and even chunks of stained glass with bearded faces of saints.

She followed the path to the bench in front of Our Lady of Grace's shrine, a brick grotto inside of which a statue of the Virgin stood looking down at the votive candles and the stone kneeler. Before the fire had ruined the church, Doreen used to sneak into the shrine with Trilly from the softball team. Crouching in the shadows during Sunday services, they smoked pot while the priest's voice droned Latin over the PA system and laughed in silent convulsions, Trilly's eyes blue and watery in the sunlight, her blond hair parted down the middle, framing her square face.

On the rides home, she sat in the backseat of the

Buick with her brother, Ellis, French music whining on the radio. Her mother sat up front wearing her pointy black-rimmed glasses attached to a silver chain. Her father's overworked hands, his knuckles the size of pecans, rested on the steering wheel. While they rode along the bayou road songs such as "Jolie Blonde" or "Marksville Two-Step" chimed out of the AM radio. Ellis fidgeted in his skinny black tie, his black wingtips, and his starched white shirt, watching the cane rows pass and worrying about the Sunday night draft lottery.

Doreen walked among the anonymous tombs. This is all life is, she decided. Like the boxes stowed in her attic, full of softball ribbons, trophies, yearbooks, medals, photographs of her mother, father, brother, grandparents, of dances with painted cardboard backdrops, and boys like Jefferson Schez, Billy Evans, Thomas Curat. Ironed hair, crew cuts, beehives, and shaggy tops. This is how life is, she thought, a blurred existence recorded in inked report cards, faded photographs, brittle letters, and faulty memories. The dead were mere relics in a box put away in graveyards and forgotten. Dressed in their finest outfits as handsome or pretty as they could be, the dead were waiting forever for God to take them away, like packages.

Doreen could feel Clayton's heels jabbing into her hips. He wanted down to run alongside his brother.

"Hold my hand, Whitty. You want to see where Maw Maw is and your brother Ferdinand? Come see. I'll show you."

But the boy stood in his blue jeans, cuffed once to his shins, and with a stick he knocked clumps of moss from the low-hanging limbs. In his other hand he held a broken brick. Doreen continued walking until finally Whitaker caught up and took her hand.

She had gone a long time without visiting the graves, until one night several months after Ferdinand died she awoke with the feeling of him inside her belly. She lay in the bed staring into the dark. Russell snored in rhythmic blasts. Whitaker slept on the floor beside her.

She quietly arose and left the house and stood barefooted on the aggregate driveway, listening to the whine of the highway and, closer, the whirring of crickets. The stars were indistinct behind a haze of clouds. When she turned back to the house, she felt a pain like a fishhook in her chest. She tried to ignore it, but it slid into the wall of her heart, stitching itself deeper and deeper until she was certain that if she didn't give in to the pulling, her heart would be torn from her chest and dragged away down the dark street.

Moments later she was in the station wagon, shoeless and shivering, the headlights shining down the bayou road. The hook pulled tighter and tighter as the glowing speedometer needle rose, eclipsing numbers: 55, 60, 65, 70.

When she reached the graveyard she parked so the car's headlights would shine across the tombs. Barefooted she walked through mud and grass until she came to Ferdinand's plot, which lay beside her mother's. She sat on the black carpet of leaves, passing her hand over the concrete vault. Only then did the intolerable pulling cease. She talked to the grave, whispering into the chill air, telling her dead family what had happened.

It was like that every night for a week. The same pulling. By the fourth night she slept on the couch with her keys on the coffee table. Just as suddenly as it had started, it ended, as if the hook had passed from her body.

As Doreen and the boys worked around the vault wall, she saw a man, thin and dark-faced, moving among the shadows of the oak trees. He squatted at a family plot facing a grave marked with a stone lamb. The man seemed to read the inscription and shake his head. He didn't look at her or the boys, and for a moment it was as if she were watching him and making him uncomfortable.

"Come on now, Whitty. Come on, *you*." He had wandered to the threshold of the family plot's wrought-iron gate where sharp fleurs-de-lis bloomed into crescents of rust. Doreen was surprised to see the sunflowers still alive. It had been a mild October though, and they could hang on into November.

"How come they are sunflowers, Momma?"

"That's just how she wanted it, Whitty."

As her mother lay in the hospital bed, she told Doreen that she wanted an oak tree planted in her chest. She had been placed on a morphine drip and woke from a dream to tell Doreen that she dreamed an oak tree grew out of her, and the children played in the tree for years and years. "Promise me," she had slurred. Thrust by the morphine into the final strait between life and whatever comes after it.

"Who's buried here?"

"No one."

"What's that say?"

"Ferdinand Gidot. That's Paw Paw. He's my daddy. That's where we'll put him when he dies. If they don't make us go to the new church like they did to everybody else."

She saw movement among the tombs again. Hardly anyone came to the graveyard anymore. In the old section of Maringouin, it was surrounded by a cluster of tumbledown shacks with parish signs that prohibited entry, but people who rode the interstate, drug addicts, and drifters, were rumored to hole up there.

After Grace Church had burned, a new Catholic church, Immaculate Conception, was built in town. A low brown ranchlike structure with exposed cedar beams running beneath a spiritless geometrical ceiling. The Catholic Church had declared that the tombs should be moved to the new churchyard, but no one really wanted to do this. No one wanted to exhume the dead, and no one wanted them on the grounds of the new church. It was too much work, too much money, and the LaFont family claimed the money they gave was for the living, not the dead. They had big money from renting old cattle land to the oil companies. None of their family was buried at Grace.

Doreen set the toddler on a spread afghan and took

a rag out of the purple bucket she had purchased at the TG&Y. She began to clean the grave in sweeping motions, stretching her body across the slate and marble. Clayton lay like a pasty frog, gazing at the sky as leaves drifted slowly down around him.

"Look in there, Whitty, in that locket. That's a medaillon de vivre. It's a picture of the person in the grave." She remembered as a girl flicking open such chrome lockets that were attached to tombs and seeing black and white photographs of the dead in them. The photograph of her mother had been taken on the day of her parents' wedding. They had eloped. Standing at the water's edge of a bayou in a knee-length dark dress, Doreen's mother gazed out at the camera, trapped for eternity in a small locket frame. A young girl with a French braid in her hair and a stray dog lapping water from the bayou behind her.

Whitaker opened the locket. "How old was she?"

"She was eighteen."

"She was pretty."

"Yes, she was pretty."

"I'd have liked her I bet."

"You would have liked her, Whitty."

"What did you look like when you were eighteen, Momma?"

She rubbed the worn marble edge of the tomb's basin. Blue and green striations emerged from the gray film.

"I don't know."

* * *

We cleaned the vault graves of my family. My mother. My grandfather and all the uncles and cousins. It's strange how so many people used to come and clean their family's graves every year on this day, but now they don't. They've all forgotten, I guess.

The sun came across the trees when we were done. I had put the cleaning supplies back in the bucket and picked up Clayton, who had been asleep on the afghan. I was standing outside the waist-high gate of the family plot when I saw him. Clayton was still asleep in my arms. Whitaker stood beside me.

He was a shock to me. I hadn't seen him for hours and was sure he had left the cemetery. But he was standing there looking at me from behind an oak, his face covered by a wad of tree moss. He had draped it across his eyes which were fixed on me. His hands were hidden behind the tree.

I eased Clayton to the ground and tried to take Whitaker's hand, but he was still holding the broken brick he had picked up earlier. I threw the bottle of 409 at the man, who did not budge. Whitaker looked up at me, his eyes questioning.

I wanted to pick my boys up and run to the road, stop a car maybe, but it was too far to go. Without thinking, I took the chunk of brick from Whitaker's hand, and calculating the distance to the man, I rose to my feet. He stepped from behind the tree and moved toward me. Stepping forward, I whirled my arm in the arc I had drawn in the air so many times in high school and released the brick in one perfect movement. He stopped, as if he thought the brick would go past him, but it struck his face, and he collapsed in a heap on the ground.

I drew up the boys in my arms and ran to the car, tossed them both into the backseat. Clayton burst out crying, but it didn't matter. We were in the car. I started the engine and looked toward the cemetery. I couldn't see anyone. Just light bathing the graves.

* * *

Violet Diddier Gidot crouched on the floorboard of her stepfather's El Camino Classic and did not move a muscle. She was the adopted daughter of Ellis Gidot. A child brought into the world by his wife and her previous husband. A child of whom he was legally the father, but nothing more. Three hours had passed since her father had left her saying, "Violet, baby, I'm just going inside for thirty minutes. I'll be right out."

"You're not going to stay in there long?"

"No, baby. Thirty minutes tops. I'll put your Buckskin Bill songs on, and by the time they finish, I'll be back. I promise. Daddy loves you." He kissed her on the forehead.

But he hadn't returned in thirty minutes. So she stayed in the car, doors locked, head down. And the eight-track player blasted sing-along songs over and over.

The El Camino was parked at an angle across two spaces in front of the Lucky Spot Café and Truck Stop, a wood plank structure added onto so many times, creating so many makeshift rooms and lean-tos, that it sprawled across the entire lot, a dilapidated maze beneath the highway lights.

People on their way out of the building had spotted Violet in the passenger seat and tried to get her to open the door. Drunk people, men and women who meant no harm, but she feared them and crawled to the floorboard, trying to get out of view. Still they tapped on the window, men with stubby fingers and women with painted press-on nails, smudging their noses against the glass.

"What the hell's she listening to?"

"Sounds like hillbilly music or something."

"She'll go deaf from it fore too long."

It wasn't hillbilly music but an eight-track recording from her favorite television show, *Buckskin Bill's Sing Along*, and it had eight songs including "The Monday Morning March," "An Elephant and a Flea," and her favorite, "You Are My Sunshine." The triangle and the kazoo rang the El Camino like the parish church bell, and Buckskin Bill's voice along with a guitar and banjo—two of the most consoling sounds she'd known up to that point—had become a terrorizing net beneath which she felt trapped.

Eventually a woman of the group would go inside trying to find Violet's stepfather and then, without him, come back and drag the drunken group off to their own cars or trucks or tractor-trailers.

It was Doreen Bueche, driving straight up the highway, who happened to notice the familiar yellow El parked in the lot, and turned the station wagon around, jostling her sleeping boys against the doors. Parking the car at the Lucky Spot, Doreen walked briskly toward the El Camino, where she saw Violet crouched on the floor. Music vibrated the car doors.

"Goddammit, he did it again." Doreen knocked on the glass. "Violet, unlock the door. Violet?" The girl did not raise her head. "Violet, I'll be right back."

Doreen searched the Lucky Spot. Each room was full of card tables with men sitting about them and televisions with horses running across their screens. The barroom was lit only by neon lights. Slips of paper littered the brick floors. She waded through the greasy smell of deep-fried oysters, catfish, crawfish and shrimp and potatoes, the sour smell of spilled beer. Finally she came upon a small yellow room with a red felt pool table in it. Water stains from the leaking roof made strange faces on the walls, each one labeled with a wide black marker: *Dolly Parton, Burt Reynolds, Richard Nixon, Jimmy Carter*.

Her brother slouched in a corner of the room beneath a stain labeled *Elvis*. Passed out in an old dinner chair. Drunk and delivered. Blue jeans tucked into his snakeskin boots, pool cue between his legs, a stream of saliva down his chin. Doreen knelt and worked his key ring off a belt loop, then moved past the men who stood in ten-gallon hats, mouths gaping. By the time they thought of something sleazy to say, she was gone.

She opened the door and shut off the tape player. Violet's straw-blond hair drifted back, and her dark brown eyes gazed up at Doreen.

"Violet. I'm taking you to my house. We'll call your momma. Is there anything you want to take with you?"

Violet pointed at a cloth angel with paper clothes. Doreen lifted the girl up to her hip and bumped the car door closed with her rear end. Back in the station wagon Clayton cried and Whitaker watched, his face a small pale oval in the darkness.

"My momma's in Cancún," Violet said.

"What about your daddy?"

The diminutive girl raised her shoulders, a perfect mock performance of the same gesture her mother made when asked of Violet's real father's whereabouts.

"Then you'll stay with us tonight."

When Doreen got home, the phone was ringing. The three children followed her into the kitchen like small fish follow a bigger fish. Dishes and silverware were strewn across the counter. The table was covered with old newspapers, magazines, and TV guides so that it had ceased to be a kitchen table and become a chaotic repository of the printed word—daily, picayune, and outdated information. She caught the phone on the sixth ring.

"Russell? Oh, Russell. Where are you?" The children's eyes were fixed on her. After she had gotten back into the car at the Lucky Spot, they had been as silent as little dolls, watching, listening, or else closing the world off completely. "Russell, you don't know what we been through today. I can't come get you. I can't put the kids back in the car. My brother left Violet in the parking lot again. I stopped and got her. She's staying with us tonight."

He told her that he'd find a ride home from the plant. He'd wait till nine-thirty when an eighteen wheeler was taking off for Texas with a tanker full of chemicals.

"Call Daddy. He'll come get you. I'll be up waiting for you. We need to talk before you leave."

She fit Clayton into his old crib in her bedroom and told Whitaker and Violet to stay in the house while she took a nap. "Just a fifteen-minute nap," she said, her head already cloudy. She turned on the boxy AM radio beside the bed and lay back as a woman's voice rose and fell beneath crackles like fireworks across a black sky.

The woman sang of painted swings on a fairground and March winds that could make a heart dance. She sang of a ghost and of foolish things. Doreen saw couples dancing in empty kitchens and dancehalls as the words of the singer went into her. Then she was in a small room, dull with pewter walls and hammered lead floors. Ferdinand lay outstretched in a perfect white gown, his face and hands copper and densely metallic. She sat on the floor and petted his head. Then she slept, deeply, motionlessly, completely.

* * *

Violet stood in the corner of my room holding her cloth angel, her lip curved down. There was something about the arc in her lip, something mathematical and spirited, like arcs in the Roman aqueducts or the Gateway Arch in Saint Louis or the palladium windows at the New Orleans bus station.

She pointed to the poster above my bed—a man with a mustache and dark hair in a New York Yankees uniform. He leaned forward in that anticipatory moment after he has done all he could with the ball and now waits for that other moment when it is caught or rockets back into the field.

"That's Ron Guidry."

I drew my finger across his name, written in white across a patch of shadow beneath him and looked back at her. She was staring at the poster, twisting the yellow yarn of the doll's hair with her index finger.

"He's Louisiana Lightning. He's Cajun like us."

Violet's eyes moved back and forth from me to the poster.

"I wrote him a letter. He never wrote me back."

She walked toward the window.

"You wanna go down to the pier? I'll show you something."

She nodded, and I opened my bedroom window and dipped my bare feet into the cypress mulch of my mother's garden. In the spring the fruit tree bowed toward my window, heavy with yellow Japanese plums. Mint grew wild about the cement stepping stones, orchids drew up bold orange faces, and hummingbirds hovered in suits of green feathers. But then, in November, ladybugs had collected on the brick sill after flicking themselves hopefully at the glass.

Our brick house was built in the 1960s on the ruined grounds of an old river cabin. The house suffered from an architectural split personality. It had traits of a ranch house—low ceiling, long Bauhaus windows, and earth-toned bricks—but it also mimicked features from the old Acadian cabin that came before it—a gable roof, children's stairs on the gallery, and a long wood porch that faced the Lac Coupee.

Below the slanting levee, the Lac Coupee ran—and still runs—twenty miles of oxbow lake as wide as the Mississippi River, to which it was once linked. Sometime in the 1800s, the northern mouth of the oxbow closed during spring rains, and the river moved east. Since then, the people who have lived along Lac Coupee cherish their heritage of isolation, their community that nurses at the stagnant waters, the yellow and dismal reek of Lac Coupee's drink.

"Come see," I said from outside the window. I took from my pocket a handful of firecrackers and a box of wooden matches. "I got these. They're little bombs. We'll explode em."

"Aunt Doreen said not to go outside," Violet said.

"She won't care."

She followed me out the window as I unlatched the gate beside the cement fountain—a peasant boy and girl forever spilling the contents of a cement vase. Down at the pier behind the house *poule d' eaus* churned in the water, diving and reemerging to swallow small fish. The birds honked like bicycle horns as we tramped the musty wood of the pier, then swam away from us out toward the last light.

"I like those birds," Violet said, giggly.

"Those are trash birds," I said.

"I still like them."

We walked past the bushes where Angel Boy had fallen. At the center of the pier a dead catfish lay. Violet stopped beside me. The catfish's head was preserved, rolled in bits of mud and stems. Beneath the gills and the gray rubbery flesh was the skeleton, a sophisticated configuration like the architecture of a suspension bridge.

"What is it?"

"Catfish."

"What does that to it?"

"Nutria rat does it. They pull the fish up on the pier at night and eat em. I'd like to fish up a nutria rat and kill it. Bully McGovern and them go out in his daddy's bateaux at night. They tape flashlights to pellet guns and shoot nutria rats. I'm going with them next year. You better not walk in the high grass at night with no shoes on. My daddy tells me nutria rats eat your toes."

"Nuh-uh."

"Yes, they will. They eat dogs and cats too." The idea terrified me. "What do you want to explode?"

"I don't have anything to explode." Violet held up her angel. "How bout this? You could explode this."

"That's your baby doll."

"I know," she said, staring out over the water. "I don't care about it."

I lay it on the pier. "It's a pretty little thing," I said.

"I don't care," she said again.

I told Violet to stand at the end of the pier while I fixed the M-80 inside the doll's legs. I broke two kitchen matches and tossed the sticks into the water. When I finally lit the firecracker and dashed back to her, Violet started to cry. She bolted toward the doll.

"Don't!" I grabbed her shirt as the firecracker exploded, a quick stupid crack. Bits of cotton and synthetic fibers hovered in the air and floated down to the water.

Violet curled up on the pier cupping her ears. I stood over her saying, "Hey. Hey. Hey."

My mother came to the screen door, Clayton wailing in her arms.

She brought Violet some Kool-Aid, and I had to pick up pieces of the doll, wading out into the lake with my pants rolled high and the mud slimy between my toes. My mother tried to get Violet to throw it all away, but she wouldn't, so we sat on the wooden floor of my bedroom and tried to stitch the doll back together. But it was useless. We put the pieces of the doll in a plastic sandwich bag.

That night we all slept in Momma and Daddy's room, Clayton in his crib, me and Momma and Violet in the bed. Violet slept with the plastic bag in her arms. I pulled her hand over my head and went to sleep.

* * *

Russell Ulysse Bueche did not sleep that last night in Maringouin. He had come home late and gone to the guest room so as not to wake Doreen and the children. His head was sick with numbers, infested with digits. He lay wide-eyed, working out the bills, interest payments, paychecks, trying to figure out a way to make the numbers work, trying to fix it so he wouldn't have to take the freighter job again.

Doreen's father, old Ferdinand Gidot, had picked Russell up at the plant, and he worried that the old man would ask about him and Doreen and the kids and why he was leaving. But he didn't. He didn't say much of anything as they drove down the highway, everything dark but the asphalt in front of them and Ferdinand's face in the glow of the instruments.

When Doreen was sick he had let her make up the room any way she wanted. Pink curtains, sky-blue walls, ribbons and trophies from high school on the desk, photos from their wedding, pictures of her with the kids in their Easter outfits, records and romance novels on the shelves.

This night was like the nights when they would fight and he would sleep in this room. He wasn't getting away from her at all though. The room was a museum of her, the pillows scented with her perfume. It was as if he were trapped inside her. Russell stared at the ceiling with the blankets pulled up to his chin until the sun came up.

His airline tickets lay on the coffee table in the living room. He showered and dressed, picked up the tickets and slung his duffle bag across his shoulder. The house was quiet and still. He checked on Doreen, but she was still asleep, the children gathered around her, Whitaker on one side, his head at her hip, and Violet on the other with a plastic bag under her arm, her head against Doreen's side. He removed his blue glasses and rubbed his eyes, the room swooning until he put them back on.

He went over to the crib and kissed the baby on his forehead. Clayton's brown eyelashes fluttered, but his eyes did not open. Then Russell was out the door, his duffle bag over his shoulder. He wished she'd have seen him off as he waited for the car.

"You were going to leave without saying goodbye?" he imagined her saying.

"I don't know. I wasn't thinking."

"I'm going to miss you."

"No you won't." He always said something stupid at critical moments.

"I will."

"I'll send along the checks through the service. They say you can go and pick them up at the plant office."

"You don't have to leave."

"Yes I do. I'll do no good here. I know if I stay on too long something will go off inside me. If it goes off I'll be no good to them and to you. That's the best I can describe it, Doreen."

But that was not real. He could not say how he felt.

As the airport taxi came down the street he was certain he was forgetting something. When he got into the stale-smelling taxi and started making chitchat with the driver, his heart started pounding and he could hardly breathe. He rolled down the window to feel the cold air. His lungs hurt and his belly ached for fire and food and the smells of the house on the lake in Maringouin.

Bosporus 1984

THEY WILL NOT LET YOU SMOKE ON THE ship. The night before, when we were pitching back and forth, I couldn't sleep. When that happens, I go up, hustling aft along the steel passageways, each step flat and balanced. I cradle a cigarette in my palm. Captain Nichos has good reason for not letting us smoke. The freighter carries jet fuel, which we haul from Galveston, Texas, to air force bases in Europe and Israel.

I'd been on and off such ships for more than four years, and my time aboard was a dream of cold iron and electric light, of drunken chatter, and hours watching maintenance screens under the hangover haze, and off time—home a month or two at a stretch, going through the motions of being a father and a husband and not feeling like anything but a fill-in for somebody else.

This was the third night I couldn't sleep. I kept seeing a guy drowning, lost in those ice-cold waters. Hanover started me on it. I didn't think about this crap until I met Hanover.

"It happens all the time. Some deckhand gets swept over in a gale. No one knows about it for a day. And by then . . ." Hanover would make that face, shrug his shoulders. He hams it up cause he knows it disturbs the bejesus out of me.

Hanover. The ship doctor. We share berth eight. Two fold-down cots and a stainless-steel desk. Lucked out. When I go to smoke, I can't wake him. He snores all night, his face lit by the low-watt glow of the neon-green wall lights running along the bulkhead. He wears a beard, not an ordinary beard. It's black and cone-shaped, an upside down Christmas tree stopping at his tie clip. Hanover always wears a khaki military uniform—trousers, shirt, and tie. At first I figured it was a nautical doctor's getup, but he wears no patches or insignia. He said that Texaco doesn't make him wear any uniform at all. He likes wearing it out of "personal choice."

I asked him one night if he was a real doctor.

"Yes, I am." He was sitting at the fold-down desk in our room.

"Why are you working such a shit job as this?" He took off his glasses. His eyes always looked like he was falling asleep. He was reading a book written in Greek, or Russian maybe. Hanover petted his beard like it was a lapdog.

"It's all I can manage for now."

"A doctor on a damned tin can? I bet you could do better. Most of these rat floats don't even have doctors."

"I needed to get away. Time to myself. Time for my theory. My book."

When we were docked in San Sebastian, Hanover got drunk and started to tell me how he had this accident at a hospital. He got all worked up, and I told him to shut up. I didn't want to know what he did. Now it's one of those things we don't talk about. He might not even remember, and I'd rather keep it that way. I don't want to have something on Hanover. That's how things get shitty on a boat, when you have something on somebody else.

That's why, when I come back down from my smoke on deck, I shower. I go to the head and scrub myself down until my hair, my skin reeks of Dial. That way no one will rat me out. You get five hundred bucks for ratting somebody out for smoking. I bet Captain Nichos carries five crisp Franklins around in his trouser pocket. Everybody starts to look more and more like rats every day.

On the freighter I check gauges. I radio the bridge from the engine room. I toss out lines from the deck in port. I do what they tell me and never speak to Captain Nichos unless he speaks to me first. He's a short prick. A Greek-American with a little-man complex.

In Istanbul the harbor pilot boarded. He was a smooth-looking Turk in a wool jacket and a camel's-hair scarf. I was on the bridge, watching the smoke levels on the monitor. Then the harbor pilot's radio went off, and the radio voice started yelling in Turkish. Turned out we couldn't dock for another day. He offered to take some men in. A few of us got a hotel in the city for the night. Donald and Wayne, Heap, Hanover, and me.

We rode a tug across the choppy spits of the Bosporus until the docks emerged on the European side of the city. We got hassled over our passports on the quay by some cops with semiautomatic machine guns, then took a bus into the city.

The hotel we stayed at was pretty nice. The view from the rooms was good. More mosques than you ever wanted to see. The rooms were ratty but the lobby and the bar were decked out in marble. I ordered Jim Beam with water but didn't get it. You can hardly get regular bourbon in Turkey or Greece either. All they have is Four Roses, and it was good enough with water. But I like my drinks real sweet, so I poured a couple sugar packets in and stirred it. The bartender saw me and shook his head.

"American," he said, pursing his lips.

"No shit," I said, standing up, and he backed off real quick. That's how some of these guys are. They get pissy about you, but they back off quick. Or pull knives.

Maybe it's my glasses. I wear these blue prescription lenses, had to wear them since I was a kid. My dad whacked the crap out of me once and it ruined my vision. People look funny at you when you wear blue glasses indoors. Trust me. If I don't wear them my eyes get these weird cramps, and my vision blurs and bends. My head feels like tin and the light bangs it.

Hanover came out of the elevator. He's a strange bird to look at. You'd really have to see him. I was almost embarrassed that he was coming to sit down with me. He had on his uniform, pressed and creased, and it always made me think of the old cavalry movies when they would rip a soldier's patches off if they thought he didn't belong. He carried a notebook, the one he'd been writing in.

"So what are you writing anyway, Hanover?"

He sat down, adjusted his plain tie, called for the bartender.

"White wine, sir," Hanover said. The bartender nodded.

"It's a book about dolphins."

"Fish and shit."

"No, Russell, not fish and shit. Dolphins." He looked like I'd just pissed on his precious notebook.

"Seriously, I want to know."

The bartender looked sideways at me as he set the wine on the little glass table and went away.

"It's based on the idea that we are cousins with the dolphins."

"Go on."

"You know the story of evolution, right? In a nutshell, we were once sludge that evolved into sea life that crawled up on the shore. And we evolved differently to meet the terrain. We had to adjust to the land."

"All right."

"I believe that dolphins are our cousins. They are the us that stayed behind in the water. So it's like the ships we ride are spaceships to them. We cruise on the outer sphere of their world. That's why they try to make contact with us. To explain it all. But the thing is they've evolved differently, so it's difficult to communicate. They are nicer than we are too. Better because they didn't get too mean and have to adapt as much as us. They are still curious about the land and us and how we managed, but they never let their desire for other things get the best of them. So I believe they are more content. They didn't have to scrape and fight and change *as much*. Of course that doesn't make them more powerful does it? It makes us more powerful."

"And you really believe all that?"

He took a sip from his glass holding it at the stem and watched the bartender walk away from the lounge. He ran his palm across his beard. It was four o'clock, and another bartender came on duty.

"I know it sounds crazy to someone like you, Russell. But it's my idea."

"I didn't say you were crazy." I thought about it. "I don't care for science. Science is shit."

We sat there for a while. American music came from somewhere behind the bar. Shit like when I was a little kid. Elvis. Motown. I wanted them to turn it off.

"That music reminds me of home. How far do you have to get away to get away?" I said.

Hanover shrugged like he always does. "We carry our demons with us, they say."

The new bartender came over. He gave us the drinks we ordered. Some of the other guys from the freighter came down on the elevator. Spic and span. Ready for a night on the town. They asked us if we wanted to go out. Donald and Heap. "I'm gonna stick around here with Hanover for a while. We'll catch up."

I thought about going off with the other guys, but that always felt like being alone with guys who were just like me, and that was no good. Hanover made me uneasy but at least there was a give and take with him. He kept on about his book. I watched some women in pink dresses parade into the lobby and down the steps into a wedding party beyond the bar.

"I didn't know women could wear dresses like that over here."

"Istanbul is quite cosmopolitan, Russell. Quite cosmopolitan."

I looked up at the clock. Subtracted some numbers.

"I'm gonna go call my kids, Hanover. I think they should be just waking up right now in the States. I want to call them."

"You're drunk already."

"No I'm not. I just want to call them."

I went across the lobby. The floor was green and rich looking. With a few drinks in me I was all of a sudden kind of happy. I called the kids on the pay phone under the stairwell. I told them I was going to take them fishing when I got home. I always tell them I'll take them fishing when I got home. Sometimes I do, sometimes I don't. I talked to my wife. She was feeling good, which was good to hear. I told her I loved her. It's easy to tell her I love her when I'm drunk and in Turkey. I told her and the kids that joke about the monkey and the fireman, the only one I can remember when I'm drunk. And maybe because I was drunk and all the grief between us was out of my head, she liked me for a second. She laughed anyway. The kids laughed. I was a goddamned champion for five minutes.

When I went back up I saw the bartender standing in the center of the lobby between the red plush ottomans and the check-in desk. A woman behind the front desk was speaking to him. The bartender put a hand to his forehead as if remembering something. And then he lowered both hands down at his sides and fell—smack—to the floor.

I stopped by the marble column to see him better. He was wearing a silver-gray suit, and he had the look that little Ferdinand had. Like whatever he was looking at was the same thing Ferdinand had been looking at. One guy knelt down to check him, then vomit started coming out of the bartender's mouth. The guy started to pump on his chest. He called out in Turkish to the two girls behind the desk. They had on blue blazers. Their hair was pulled up, and silk scarves draped their necks. The prettier woman ran off and returned with the manager of the hotel. A middle-aged guy in a nice suit, specks of gray in his hair. He spoke with an English accent.

"Doctor?" he said to the man pumping on the bartender's chest. The man felt for a pulse, shook his head, and said something I couldn't understand. Then he kept pumping, ignoring the manager.

"I'll get one," I said and went back to the bar, which was just around a partition from the lobby. Hanover was still at the table.

"Doctor?" I said, "There's a man down in there."

Hanover cut his eyes at me when I called him doctor. I realized it was the first time I'd ever called him that, and he looked miserable about it, that I'd pointed out he was a doctor only when a man was lying on the floor of the Aya Sophia Hotel.

"Really?" Hanover said. "I don't know if I should stay out of it. Being in a foreign country and all." But as he spoke he stood up. That's when I knew he was better than I was.

When we came around the columns, there were a couple of people looking down at the bartender as if he were something that interested them in a store window. Most of the people moving through the lobby just glanced down and kept walking as if every day they came into the Aya Sophia Hotel at four o'clock and saw a dying bartender on the floor. Hanover knelt beside him.

"Doctor?" the manager said.

"Yes. American doctor. Did somebody call an ambulance?"

"Yes," the manager said, his eyes measuring the crowd. Hanover started checking the unconscious man. He lifted his eyelids, and the bartender's eyes were fixed on nothing. There was not a pissy bartender anymore. There was no man at all. The man was gone.

Hanover rolled the bartender over, and vomit came out of his mouth.

"I need a towel. Get me a towel."

The hotel manager said something in Turkish to the women, and they pulled the pretty silk scarves from their throats. The manager clawed at the scarves and tossed them to Hanover. Hanover put the scarves over the bartender's mouth and breathed into him. He did this for a long time. Lots of people stopped and watched.

The hotel manager sent for some other men to place movable screens around the bartender. Hanover kept breathing into his mouth and the other guy kept pressing at his chest. People checked in at the desk. Some people stopped and peaked in, some moved away quickly, and others lingered, stealing glances at the sick man until one of the hotel employees pushed them along politely.

"He's dead," Hanover said. "I've got no pulse. He's dead." But still he kept pushing on the man's chest. No one spoke until the ambulance arrived twenty minutes later. The medics came in, and Hanover asked if they had a defibrillator. They shook their heads, threw the bartender on a stretcher, and jogged him to the ambulance outside. The ambulance driver was waiting by the doors, a Greek man fidgeting with those string beads that most

Greek taxi drivers carry. The driver raised his head questioningly at the man steering the bartender's body toward the vehicle.

"Thanatos," the medic said.

As we followed the medics outside, I noticed that Hanover's lips were raw. The manager apologized. He thanked Hanover and asked him to stop by the front desk later. The ambulance turned onto the avenue, but the cars were thick, so it turned around and went the other way. It was very cold outside. Like on a mountain. Suddenly we were alone.

"They would never have done it that way in America," Hanover said. "They would have stabilized him first. They wouldn't move him. Did you see the way they just threw him on the stretcher? They should have used a defibrillator first and worked on him a bit."

"Think they'll revive him? I mean, what happened you think?"

We looked off toward the shrinking taillights of the ambulance, and then they vanished in the traffic.

"It could be anything. Aneurysm. His heart could have just stopped. When the vomit comes up like that, sometimes it can run back into the lungs, and they can drown in it."

I asked if he wanted to call it a night, but he didn't. We went to the room. He washed out his mouth with Listerine. He showered. He came out of the bathroom clean and pressed. I couldn't tell if he had on a new khaki outfit or not.

"Let's go to a bar," Hanover said. "One away from the hotel. It's funny how death follows you around. I can't turn around without somebody dropping dead. I'm sick of dead people, Russell. To be honest with you."

I wanted to say something, but I didn't.

We walked on Seref Efendi Street near the Covered Bazaar, where the men had olive-colored faces, their bodies and hands stowed away in pockets and gloves, and the women's faces were covered with silk scarves. Dogs trotted around pissing on walls. As we walked along we didn't speak. I could tell Hanover was thinking about the bartender. A blind beggar tapped a cane on the cobbled road. His eyes were scars. In front of him was a plastic bathroom scale, and when passersby stepped on it he called out their weights, and they dropped coins into his wool hat upturned on the road.

We passed a small mosque jammed between two buildings. Prayers cut through the air, Arabic words projected across the city by muezzins mounted atop stone minarets which rose above the cracked walls of the courtyard. The minarets were dark and colorless against the gray winter clouds, like the smoke stacks at TEXACO back in Baton Rouge.

I took my blue glasses off to see the minarets swirl in the sky. The prayer songs echoed down the alleyway. Pigeons lit on the domes. Muslim men squatted in front of the mosques, their shoes beside them. Turning the brass spigots at the fountains, they washed themselves before pushing open the dark wooden doors. Steam rose up out of the long marble basins. I could not understand how they believed in something so much.

We took a small back table in a dark bar just a few blocks from the Bosporus Strait. Neon lights shone, and the bottles were reflected in a mirror behind the bar. Hanover started drinking. Really drinking. He had four vodkas in not much over a half-hour.

"I wonder if he had a family?" he said.

I shrugged my shoulders.

"It's possible he didn't. I don't really have any, you know."

"He seemed like an asshole to me." I said. "I'm sorry about getting you, Hanover. I should have left you out of it."

"It didn't matter. I couldn't do anything to a dead man anyway. That's one thing I couldn't screw up." He called the waitress over and ordered another round. "It's possible he was a jerk though. A misanthrope even."

"What's a misanthrope?"

"A person who hates other people."

"Oh. Well, that's what he was I bet. A misanthrope." Hanover looked me in the eye. My hands went clammy. "Well if he did have a family I bet they'd want to thank you for trying to save him. Even if you couldn't."

He didn't say anything.

"I mean. I know I would forgive you if it was my family or something that went like that and you'd tried to . . . to . . ."

I shut up. Hanover's eyes were fixed on the dark wood table.

We stayed on at the bar for a while. When I got up to piss, I thought I would fall over. It wasn't because of drinking. I didn't quite have my land legs back. Coming back to land was like stepping off the tilt-a-whirl at the state fair.

When I returned, there was money on the table. My cigarettes were gone, and so was Hanover. His jacket was folded neatly over the back of his chair. I picked it up and walked out to the street. The buildings looked wet and worn down, and steam rose from the sewer grates. I walked toward the hotel. The moon came out from the clouds and cast shadows onto the street. I came upon two kids, one bigger than the other, the big one screaming at the smaller one and walking around like a rabid dog. His voice was tattered. Finally he struck the smaller kid with an open hand, and the kid took it. I crossed the street to get away from them.

In a doorway I saw a beggar hunched over, his body a black form against the moonlit pavement. He was sobbing, his arms curled around his knees, his hands shivering knots. Then he looked up at me. Hanover.

"What the hell are you doing?" I said. "You'll freeze to death out here. I thought you were a damned bum."

Hanover grabbed my pant legs and clawed my shirt, pulling himself up from the pavement. "I need to talk to you, Russell. It was my fault. At the hospital back home. It was my fault." His cheeks were wet with tears.

"Hanover, calm down. I don't want to know. I don't want to have anything on you. You understand that?"

"Just listen. Listen to me."

"Get ahold of yourself, Hanover. Back off. Shape up. You're just drunk."

"Listen to me," he said. "Just listen. Listen." Suddenly he darted away. The tan fabric of his uniform caught the white of the streetlights as he bolted down the sloping road until I couldn't see him anymore.

"Jesus," I said. The streets were empty. The two boys were gone. I started walking fast, looking for Hanover down by the park. I called out to him, but the fog was thick and muffled my voice. As I walked on, the air got colder. The road turned sharply downward until it halted at a steep quay. Below me there was a gulping sound of water. Rocks jutted up and ships, barges passed on the strait. The fog lay ten feet high atop the Bosporus so that I could hardly see the white names of the boats painted on the dark bows. The ship names were in Greek and Russian and Arabic.

The first time I sailed I was twenty years old. I was in New Orleans on the docks and saw a word on the bow of an international cruiser. The word was alien to me. I wrote it down on a scrap of paper and put it in my billfold. I felt that if only I figured out what the word was it would do something to me, like it was the key to something I had been missing out on. I asked a few guys if they knew what it was, but they didn't. Then I thought maybe I wasn't supposed to know what the word meant. Maybe it was something like *Red Lady* or *Exxon #12*. I decided that not knowing was better because as long as I didn't know what the word was it could be anything. I still have that word written in blue ink on a receipt in my billfold.

Beyond the Bosporus was the Asian side of the city. The fog halted at the far bank, and above the fog the tall buildings were smeared with moonlight, the lines of the mosques and towers all faint and soft. I stepped down to the water where the rocks were wet and jagged. Long dark pieces of driftwood were jammed against the bank.

At the perimeter of the fog, I saw something floating in the water. Driftwood, maybe, but it seemed too buoyant for driftwood. I waded out into the water to see what I couldn't see from the rocks.

I knew it was Hanover. That he had jumped in. And all of a sudden I went crazy thinking how I could have helped him, but that I couldn't help him now. I stepped out farther into the water, the cold current grabbing at my legs, my chest, the water coming to my neck and getting in my nose. Then I could see it, a lump of sail tangled together and swollen with air. I crawled back up on the rocks and lay flat, my chest cold and heaving until I caught my breath. Then I walked back to the top of the quay. The trees were crooked and small. The road rose. I couldn't feel my legs at all as I trudged out of the fog past the police station on Kennedy Caddesi, past the shops and apartment houses shaped like shoeboxes turned on their sides.

When I got back to the hotel, the desk clerk squinted

at the trail of water I left on the marble. I took the elevator to the hotel room, and there was Hanover lying on his bed in his boxer shorts and undershirt. One of my cigarettes was burning at the corner of his mouth, and he wore his glasses low on his nose, reading a copy of the *Times of London*.

"Christ," he said, looking up from his paper. "Did you jump in the water? You're drunk, aren't you?"

"I thought you jumped in the damn strait or something."

He looked back at his paper. "I don't know what the hell you're talking about, Coonass."

"You were drunker than Jesus! You forgot already?"

"Haven't got a clue what you're talking about, Bueche. Why don't you just drop it already."

I went to the bathroom and pissed, and when I came back into the room Hanover had turned on the television. The blanket was pulled up to his chin, and he was staring at the ceiling. I went out on the balcony and slid the glass door shut behind me. He always had a television on when we were in a room in port. Had it turned to the BBC, because, he said, he felt connected to the world by it. With the glass door closed I couldn't even hear the television.

I lit a cigarette and stared back at him. The television blaring. His eyes fixed on the ceiling. Wouldn't know how to talk to somebody if he had to. He'll probably live his whole life that way, by himself with all his problems. It's an awful way to be, if you think about it.

A Fully Loaded Cadillac for Jesus
1985

THAT NIGHT UNDER THE CHURCH PEW Violet's purple dress came above her knobby knees as she squirmed along the green carpet and slithered beneath the kneeler. Yellow-white lights hung above her from the rafters on thin black metal rungs. When she looked at them and then away, a blob of light moved with her vision. Maybe the white blur that goes wherever I look is the Holy Spirit flying around the ceiling, she thought.

The lights swayed slowly. It was significant to Violet that the lights swung in a line toward her, then toward the crucifix. Back and forth in the vents' streaming air, whose influence she did not notice. Above her the congregation's upturned faces were all lit glossy by the lights.

Their arms and hands were raised to the rafters, their bodies swaying in some invisible charismatic current.

"I see a couple of new faces here tonight," Mr. LaFont droned from the pulpit. "Some of you may be wondering why we pray in tongues. The best way I ever heard it described was by the visiting evangelical preacher Reverend Gomez. A good clean Christian. A missionary. He told us words were always going to fail us when we try to talk to each other, and even when we try to talk to God. Language is made by man and is imperfect. All the churning and whirling in our hearts can't be moved out with words, and to talk to God you can't use words. It's a big flop like that, the Reverend Gomez told us. You've got to let it rush out like the mighty Mississippi, and when it comes, then he'll understand."

Violet raised her feet, the better to see her new sandals.

"Violet," her stepfather Ellis said. "Get up. You're too big for that."

At school Violet stood taller than all the boys her age. Even with her head hung she was still a good six inches taller than everyone else. On the back row of her class picture, her mop of dirty-yellow curls stood out, and her eyes shown like dabs of hardened tar. She hated her height, and her eyes. The uncles on her mother's side would say things like, "She's pretty. But she sure got those black eyes."

Violet clacked the heels of her sandals together. "Violet," Ellis whispered, but she ignored him. All deals were off since the divorce. Ellis had gotten custody of her only because of lies people had told about her mother. Because Ellis had taken care of her and her real father hadn't, and didn't want to, she was stuck with Ellis.

On Violet's first weekend visit to Baton Rouge her mother had taken her to the mall and offered her a deal. "Don't you want two pair of sandals?" she said, squinting as if to draw the correct answer from her daughter's mouth.

"Yes, Momma," Violet said.

"Well, you can get one of the Jellies sandals, or you can get two of the not-exactly Jellies that look just like the Jellies."

There was a lame lesson in this—about money or something—that Violet did not quite understand. But at Sally Richard's birthday party, when the girls lined up their sandals on the porch before they jumped in the pool, Violet could see that the labels on the inside of her shoes said Gooeys where theirs said Jellies. She tucked her shoes under her arm and carried them to the bathroom, thinking, "I don't fit in. I don't fit in." She scraped off the labels and flushed them down the toilet, then set them on their sides on the porch. All day, in a glorious fit of denial, she tried to swim and laugh and play Marco Polo. She knew that "Jellies" meant more than just a type of shoe. All the other girls were better than her because the other girls were Jellies. Violet felt like a Gooey, messed up inside and inferior. As she swam under the chlorinated water, holding her breath until she felt her lungs would burst, she pictured the other girls, standing on the porch and passing around her shoes. But when she surfaced, Mrs. Richard called for snacks, and all the other girls ran squealing inside.

"Violet," Ellis said. "Get off the floor. Now."

His face was bright in the lights. The tips of his alligator-skin boots were smooth—leather faces without features. The backs of his hands and wrists were carpeted with curly hairs. Violet had once imagined his hands to be like the hands of God, but in the yellowish light of the sanctuary they were an apelike sham. He had been a drunk, and now he was saved.

"Suit yourself," Ellis said. "Suit yourself. I'll make you go sit with the loony if you don't behave. I bet she'd like to get her hands on a little girl like you."

"What loony?" Violet said, her head popping above the pew.

From the back row Erin LaFont smiled at Violet with the look of one dreaming in bed.

Erin was thin and tall with stringy wisps of brown hair framing her face. Her shirt was shiny black polyester. A long crescent scar started at her hairline and ended at her chin. She suffered epileptic seizures, and, after running into two ditches on Highway 19, and one cow just off Highway 19, she had lost her driver's license. She had also lost, the kids said, her mind.

The first time Violet Gidot ever saw Erin LaFont was from the school bus window.

The bus had stopped, and the sunlight illuminated

smudgy handprints on the windows where the other Maringouin Elementary schoolchildren had braced themselves. Erin sat cross-legged on the asphalt shoulder of Highway 19 among the cigarette butts and dislodged chunks of pavement.

She was a strange woman—twentyish and thin, a rat nest of brown hair and the scar running down her face. She was petting the head of a dead dog, a yellow lab with no collar and ribs in distinct lines. Violet could not tell if the dog was recently dead or if it had been dead a long time, but she could see Erin's hand cupping the sad fur of the hound's skull. Violet had never seen such evident compassion, but seeing it she felt suddenly hopeful that there were grownups who acted in the ways she was afraid to act.

Then Sally Richard, with her oversized blue ribbon, comical and foppish atop her curly head of hair, pointed out the grimy bus window and yelled, "Look at Stitchface!"

The bus shifted from the weight of the children as they leaped to see. The boys had the windows down almost immediately.

"She's picking up dinner," one boy yelled.

"She's falling in love," yelled another.

"Stitchface, Stitchface, Stitchface," they chanted.

The loudest and stupidest of the boys leaned out the window and spat. But Erin kept petting the dead animal.

"That's sick, huh Violet?" Sally said. "Isn't it sick?"

Violet nodded. "Yeah, Sally. It is sick."

These days, every morning and every evening, Erin

could be seen walking back and forth from her home to her job at the Highway 19 Used Car Lot. On weekends she worked at the church, raking leaves from the rectory lawn, and, at Advent, dollying out the crèche from the rectory storage room in the morning and locking it up at night. The crèche was made of carved Italian marble, and the LaFont family had donated it, along with a new stained-glass window, as a gift of thanks to the priests for allowing them to use the sanctuary on Thursday nights. The LaFont's also paid for a surveillance system for the nativity figures, complete with a video camera and a monitor that the receptionist could keep an eye on during the day. Ellis joked about who would want a two hundred pound statue of the Blessed Virgin.

But Erin was the real guardian of the figures. She washed and scrubbed them for hours in the rectory garage, and set them up with great consideration—the infant in the middle, the shepherds behind the kings, and the mules and sheep opposite them. She placed Mary and Joseph so close to the Christ child that their proximity suggested adoration and service. Violet had watched Erin do this from the vantage of the CCD classroom, cinching the figures on the dolly with ropes to move them just so.

And even though Erin was now a fixture at the church, a volunteer, she never entered through the front doors. A year ago the priests had set a stone amid a clump of mums in the narthex along with a Virgin Mary figure, her arm pointing to the glazed granite that said, IN MEMORY OF ALL GOD'S CHILDREN MURDERED BY THE CONTINUING

HOLOCAUST OF ABORTION. Since then Erin entered the church through the dark side door between the mahogany confessionals.

More than once Erin had been arrested out by the railroad tracks for doing things Violet did not quite understand. Violet's mother said the tales people told about Erin were rumors and lies. But the stories were too much fun for the older kids at school. Violet had heard the word the other kids gave for what Erin did, and when she asked Ellis if that was what Erin had done, he got angry. Violet never said the word to him again, nor did she ask what it meant.

Mr. LaFont had told Ellis that whatever sins Erin had committed she was paying for. Though Erin was Mr. LaFont's cousin, he acted as if they weren't related, but she was a LaFont, and if not for that nobody would have put up with her. Nobody would have even allowed her in to the prayer meetings.

"What we sow, we reap ten-fold," Mr. LaFont had told Ellis.

All around Violet people raised their hands to the rafters, and their bodies waved in some invisible charismatic current as they sang "The Devil Can Sit on a Tack," the offertory hymn. Ellis's hands were outstretched, his palms up, and he swayed side to side as if scanning the rafters of the church for a signal from the Holy Spirit. Violet thought of the people in the prayer meetings as human satellite dishes, searching the room for the best reception of the Holy Ghost. Violet could tell when they found a good frequency because they'd go into an intense and senseless rambling prayer.

Prayer meetings gave people the freedom to rant and waggle their hands and cry uncontrollably, and the prayer meetings were perfect for Erin, who, Ellis said, had a screw loose. If Erin behaved in public the way she did in the church—crying and yelling and shaking her hands—she'd be tossed in a lockup, or worse, sent back to Pineville where she'd had to spend some time after her last car accident.

But if she got too rowdy, if she got "slain by the Spirit" just a little too much, Mr. LaFont took her aside and talked to her like a parent with a wild child, shaking his finger and telling her to settle down. Erin would try to fight, but Mr. LaFont told her that if she didn't do as he said he'd cut her off from the prayer meetings. People were afraid she would go into a seizure, and if Erin hurt herself that might put an end to the meetings. Nobody wanted that.

Throughout the town of Maringouin there had been a revival of interest in full gospel worship, so much of a revival that devout Catholics had left behind their old faith for the energy, simplicity, and intensity of full-gospel congregations. The wealthy Mr. LaFont was leader of the movement. He funded most of the Full Gospel Church activities, and he had arranged for them to meet on Thursday evenings at Immaculate Conception.

The parish priest, Father Sonnier, didn't approve of

the meetings in the sanctuary because of the "foolish-ness" that went on and because the meetings weren't run by the church. But Father Sonnier was a Jesuit, and grown-ups said Jesuits didn't approve of things some-times. The old priest, Father Rabelais, went to bed at seven-thirty, and he didn't care who held meetings in the church so long as they carried Bibles and didn't break anything.

Father Sonnier was particularly upset when he found out that certain members of the group were Evangelists and Baptists. Ellis had explained to Violet that being a Full Gospel or a Baptist was like being a plain Buick or a Ford, while being a Catholic was more like being a Cadillac for Jesus. To be a good Catholic, the best, meant being a fully loaded Cadillac for Jesus.

But that was before Ellis changed his mind about Catholicism and joined the Full Gospel Church. He had said to Violet as they sat outside waiting for a prayer meeting to start that the problem with being a Cadillac for Jesus was the same problem as being an actual Cadillac—there were more parts and more wires and more of a chance for everything to break down.

He inhaled on his cigarette, delivering each sen-tence on a cloud of smoke.

Exhale: "Sometimes the power windows don't work or the computer goes out because there's so much com-plex electrical stuff in it."

Inhale.

Exhale: "But to be a Baptist or a Full Gospel is like

being a clean empty truck. You never have to worry about the power windows going out because all there is is a window crank, and there's no air conditioning or other fancy stuff."

Inhale.

Exhale: "You just ride in the clean cool air that was made by God, without having to use that fake air."

At the close of "The Devil Can Sit on a Tack," Mr. LaFont raised his arms from behind the podium, his bald head a glaring knob. His wife watched him from the front row with great admiration, as if he were president of the United States. On the strap of her leather handbag, Mrs. LaFont carried a cylinder of mace dangling from a key chain that read "Christ's Flame Church, Lee Avenue: Turn or Burn!" The LaFont's had attended Christ's Flame Church before they started the Full Gospel Church.

Mr. LaFont called his wife up to give the offertory prayer. She was small and soft-spoken and dressed in a neat blue dress with a patterned scarf around her neck, and her shoulder pads rode ridiculously high. As usual she did not pull down the microphone, and it pointed at her forehead, and as usual no one could quite hear what Mrs. LaFont was saying except that she petitioned everyone to "pray for all the Cubans who're stuck in Cuba and can't make it out to the United States where they would be free to worship and everything else."

Violet's favorite part of the prayer meetings was the

offertory because everyone was allowed to go up to the lectern and make a prayer request. When Mrs. LaFont finished her prayer, she bobbed her head, which meant it was time for anyone to step up to the microphone. Violet was first up, as she was every Thursday. She pulled down the mike and said, as always, "I would just like everyone here to pray for my stepfather."

Ellis's face turned red as a stop sign as Violet took her seat and everyone prayed for him. She bit the inside of her cheek to keep from smiling. Though her motivation was too complex for her to understand, a sweet-rotten feeling oozed through her, as black and thick as cane syrup, and she could feel the balance of power tip in her favor.

Ellis was embarrassed because everyone could tell he was a mess after his divorce and she was just an innocent acting on his behalf, drawing prayers from the communal well to salve his emotional wounds caused by the divorce.

He stood beside Violet, not praying with the others but looking off at the stained-glass windows.

After the prayer requests and the offering Mr. Percy took out his guitar and began strumming. Violet could hear Erin behind her, making loud high-pitched squeals. Violet turned around and saw Erin standing with every joint straight and locked, her arms raised toward the ceiling.

Violet nudged her father.

"What?"

"Listen to her."

"Well, go tell Mr. LaFont." He looked to the rafters and tried to find his way back into the song.

Violet walked up to Mr. LaFont in the first row. A small coffee stain in the shape of a blurry pyramid decorated the midriff of his starched blue shirt. She pushed up on her tiptoes and whispered Erin's name, and his face flushed. "I've had enough of this," he said.

Mr. LaFont's bald head glared, reflecting the overhead lights as he moved toward Erin, grabbed her arm and dragged her toward the side door. As they passed, Violet heard Mr. LaFont say, "You stay here, young lady. I'll drive you home after the meeting."

"But I didn't do anything," Erin pleaded.

Mr. LaFont returned, miffed, to his pew. "Hallelujah!" was still rolling out of Mr. Percy's guitar, but now a repetitive beat rolled along with it as Erin banged her fists against the side door, her face framed in the small glass window.

Violet told Ellis she had to go to the bathroom. Her heart pounded as she walked out the front doors of the church. The air was crisp and the lawn dark, except for rectangles of yellow light and cuts and slivers of purple and blue and red, all cast down from the stained-glass window onto Erin's back. She was breathing heavily, talking to herself in long unintelligible expostulations. Violet skirted behind the crèche, the grass cold and wet on her sandaled feet as she stepped back into the landscaped beds of azalea bushes. She surveyed the path Erin had made across the lawn, dark patches where her footprints had disturbed the wet blades.

Suddenly Violet felt bad watching Erin pace back and forth in the stained-glass light. Bad in the way she felt after squeezing the cat so hard it would yelp. Bad in the way she would sit on the roof and watch the old lady next door and want to spit on her.

"Erin! Erin! Come here."

Her mouth quivering, Erin turned.

"Come here."

Erin stepped cautiously from the darkness toward Violet.

"Guess what?"

Her shoulders twitching, Erin shook her head.

"They sent me out to tell you. To tell you you can go back in. They said they're sorry for being so rotten. They love you. They love you, and it's their fault. There's nothing wrong with you, they said. It's them."

Erin glanced down to the wet grass, then looked back at Violet. Violet could see the anxiousness in Erin's face. She looked like a cadaver Violet had seen in a documentary on television late one night. The scientist in the film ran electric currents through a dead man's face to show how the nervous system was electric. In response the cadaver made grotesque and comical grimaces.

Something inside Violet told her to shut up, told her no good could come of what she was saying, but she could not seem to stop. "They said they want you to be the new one. The new leader because you're so full of the Holy Spirit."

Violet turned away in shame, but Erin grabbed her and shook her so hard that one of her Gooeys fell with a soggy slap to the grass. Then Erin released Violet and ran around the corner of the church.

Violet jumped up, chasing Erin around to the front doors, running so fast it seemed she was gliding, spurred on by regret and fear. Erin burst into the church, her hair streaming behind her as she shouted, "I love you too! I love you all!"

The congregation turned, gawking, and when Mrs. LaFont stepped into the aisle, Erin collided into her wiry frame like a cannonball hitting a sparrow.

Violet hurried down the side aisle past the pews, while the members of the church scrambled—bald heads, polyester pants, guitars, all flashing together in wild hysteria—after Erin.

Mr. LaFont leaped from the podium to his wife's handbag, and, tearing the red cylinder of mace from the strap, he fired a streak of venom at Erin's face.

Erin wailed, staggering through the people out into the aisle. Her makeup came down in streaks of midnight black and sapphire blue as she pawed at her eyes. Then she went down, her body trembling as if God were shaking her with his fist, before her muscles went tight as wires and her back arched.

No one moved. No one spoke.

As quickly as Erin's spasms had begun, they ceased, but for a long time she stared at the ceiling, as if she could see something high in the rafters that no one else could see. Then, with great determination, Erin stood and lurched out the front doors of the church.

A few members of the congregation stayed behind with Mrs. LaFont, who lay prone on the floor, but Violet trailed the others out onto the church portico. Erin bent down to a small figure at the edge of the nativity, a lamb, which stood stoically at attention, its head slightly turned to the baby Jesus. Then Erin lifted the lamb above her head, moving slowly toward the church. When the lamb appeared to become too heavy for her to hold up, she ran toward the stained-glass window, a gift from the LaFonts commemorating the life of Emma T. LaFont, and hurled the lamb, sending it spinning through the glass which crashed into shards of blue and red and green across the lawn.

Pure light poured out onto the grass. Erin turned again to the manger, her hands fumbling across the statues. The long side of the window had not broken cleanly, and bits of glass, all jagged and crooked, hung in the opening like the teeth of a jack-o-lantern.

Erin had another figure in her arms now. The baby Jesus. She clutched it to her chest and began to run. First across the grass and then into the brightly lit parking lot. She ran in and out of cones of streetlights. Violet could see the head of the small statue poking up over Erin's shoulder. It looked back on the church and the people as if it had been planning the whole thing, as if it were in cahoots with Erin.

Violet ran to Ellis and wrapped her arms around his waist. He looked down at her. She tried to jump up into his arms, but he wouldn't let her. More people were coming out on the lawn. Those who had been there were already recounting what had happened.

Violet realized that she was like her father now. Like all the grown-ups too. She was no better than them anymore. Then she could feel it in front of her. She could feel herself moving into it as if she were in the dark. She felt something then, felt something opening up and taking her in, and though she did not know what it was, she knew what she was not.

Stone Angel
1989

O N THE THIRD SATURDAY OF MARCH, the Bueche home was under siege with the odors of the *couchon du lait*, a suckling pig cooked in the Cajun microwave—a coffin-sized box of pine planks sheathed in layer upon layer of aluminum foil. The juices of the pig dripped through a grate into a coffee can, which, when it filled with scalding hot lard, Clayton was to dump into the lake. Every so often, he hobbled with the brimming can to the bank and dumped the sizzling fat into the water.

As an infant Clayton had had steel ribbons bolted into his white patent-leather baby booties. His feet were crooked, pointed inward as if engrossed in conversation with each other. The braces were intended to straighten his soft, malleable baby bones. Years later his father said, in reference to the sulking oddness of the boy, "If only they had braces to put on that boy's head." Of course they didn't, and anyway the braces on Clayton's legs were for the most part ineffective. At age eleven his feet were still slightly crooked and his gait was a shambling back and forth, like an elegant chimpanzee.

So it was rough going, climbing the natural levee to the house, and on each trip he paused to rest at the stone that marked the spot where his twin brother had died. Above the stone was a statue of a cherub, it eyes fixed on the cypress gallery arching overhead, its angel face stupid and perfect.

Here is the place our Ferdinand passed to Heaven.
We miss him dearly, our little Angel Boy.
Love—Mom, Dad, Whit, and Clayton.

Clayton shuddered. He did not care for the sight of the angel. He did not care to think about his dead twin. He did not remember Ferdinand, nor did he remember Ferdinand's death. His parents had told him that Ferdinand had a weak heart. He had collapsed and fallen. There was nothing anyone could do.

Clayton clambered back to the house and put the can back under the oven. In the yard rose the scent of boiling crawfish. Men hunched over a cooking pot, their faces sweating and scowling, grimaces fit for the spires of cathedrals. The fire licked at the stainless steel drum inside of which crustaceans boiled, rolling and tumbling among the onions, garlic cloves, and small new potatoes.

Newspaper-covered tables sitting end to end were crowded with people who shouted over the tinny music blaring from the house. They ate from great heaps of crawfish, choosing carefully the fattest ones, plucking them up, and cracking their crimson armor to suck out the piquant meat. Heads down, eyes focused, they made the meal seem like a factory job, as if they were sorting products on a conveyor belt, examining and selecting, then moving on to the next item.

Clayton passed the people at the tables and went on in the house. On the stereo turntable spun one of his mother's records. *Blonde on Blonde.* Bob Dylan. Clayton picked up the album jacket. Dylan's face was out of focus, a checkered scarf around his neck, his hair twirled up as if he'd sat under the dryer at a beauty parlor. The music put Clayton in mind of some leaky, dismal firelit room in a distant city—Rome, New York, Babylon.

The music was nothing like what used to be played at these family gatherings. Clayton remembered old-timers sitting on the porch with fiddles and guitars and accordions. They wore polyester pants and butterfly collars, and their faces were set and grim, but their feet tapped as they sang and hollered and crooned. Most of the old French musicians were in nursing homes now. All gone now.

Clayton's brother walked past the window with Violet Gidot. Whitaker had been talking about getting out of Maringouin, and he and Violet had often argued about the possibility of his leaving. Violet thought

Whitaker was being a silly dreamer. Nobody ever got out of Maringouin. Clayton followed them outside as they walked on down the levee to the water until his father called him back to the makeshift oven where he was sifting coals.

"Is that Clayton?" a man beside his father said. "C'mere son. You recognize me? I used to live just down the road. Used to play with you and your brother. Your brother Whitaker. You remember?"

Clayton shook his head.

"This is your cousin Harold," Clayton's dad said. "Second cousin anyhow."

"Oh."

"You growing up all right," Harold said.

"Thank you."

"Say thank you, *sir*, Clayton."

"Thank you, sir."

"He little Ferdinand's brother, right?" Harold said. "The twin."

"He is," Clayton's father said, and he looked off down the levee.

"Ferdinand died," Clayton said. "He had a heart condition."

"Is that right?" Harold said, and he cast a queer glance at Clayton's father.

"You're excused now, Clayton," his father said, busying himself with the coals.

"Yes, sir."

As Clayton walked away he looked back to see the

two men whispering, but he could not make out what they said over the patois racket that made all his relatives seem ignorant and unimportant. None of them had ever been on an album cover, none of them had ever been to New York. None of them had ever been anywhere but here.

Clayton wanted to leave too, but he didn't know where he would go.

Sometimes he felt responsible for Ferdinand's death, though he never knew quite why he felt this way. Maybe it was just that he felt some guilt that he was still alive and Ferdinand was not. Sometimes he knew people whispered about his dead brother behind his back.

On his way back down the levee Clayton passed the side tables. The white porcelain plates were empty except for scraps of *boudin* with green pepper and meat, and a few blackened chunks of sausage around which flies had gathered. The empty plates made his heart feel empty. He turned and went to the house.

Clayton crouched in the broom closet. He often hid there as a small boy, and lately he liked to stuff his gangly body back into the cramped space where he'd once fit so comfortably. He took a flashlight and shined it on the cracking lacquered wall. Turning the flashlight in circles allowed him temporary status as a god of his own universe. Dust motes became the Milky Way. He heard a clatter in the kitchen. Two men were opening and slamming drawers.

"Where's the opener?"

"I don't know."

Clayton recognized the voice of his cousin Harold. The other man spoke in that distinct harbor voice of an inhabitant of Algiers or Chalmette.

"You know bout these people here?" Harold said.

"What you mean?"

"Hold on. Let me check the hall." Clayton heard Harold's footsteps as he checked the passageway. "They lost the little one."

"The boy. Yes. I think my wife said something—"

"The one that walks crooked done it."

"How you mean?"

"Apparently he knocked him down and the kid cracked his head open. They was just little, a year or so I think."

"Jesus, that's horrible."

"No kidding. His daddy, Russell, said the boy don't even know bout it. Could you imagine havin to live with dat?"

"I wouldn't want to know."

"No good in his knowing. You right on that, padnah."

The drawers opened and shut.

"Here's the damn thing. There," he said. The bottle tops clattered to the floor and the men were gone.

Around dark his mother came into his room and sat beside him on the bed. "Mom?" he said.

She put his hand on his leg. "Yeah?"

"Cousin Harold said I killed Ferdinand."

"He's lying," she said, but then she shook her head and looked out his window toward the water. "He's not lying. But I want to tell you something. You were only a baby. And nobody blames you. We were gonna tell you someday but were just waiting for the right time, and we didn't think the right time had come yet. We thought we oughta wait until you were older."

Clayton stared at a toy soldier grinning madly on the shelf.

"It was an accident. You bumped Ferdinand, and he fell, and he hit his head, and that was that. Your daddy and I are thankful we still have you, okay? Don't ever think it was your fault, okay? Promise me? Promise me you won't?"

He promised.

A few weeks after the family gathering Clayton crept from bed one night and took a hammer from the shed. He sneaked down to the cypress grove and stood before the little statue and stared a long time at its perfect stupid angel face, which was pale and accusative in the moonlight. Then he beat the angel into pieces—nose, ears, the feathery blades of its angel wings—and he took the pieces and dug a hole with the claw end of the hammer and covered the pieces over with soft earth somewhere back in the cypress grove.

No one ever asked him what happened to the

statue. And no one ever replaced it. Their father said that he bet some boys in a boat had come and taken it, something that was prone to happen when one lived along a waterway.

#1 Dad of the Galaxy 1989

RUSSELL AND HIS SON CLAYTON SAT AT the kitchen table most of the morning with two fishing rods propped expectantly by the sliding glass door. The nylon lines were taut on the reels. Alongside the rods a white ice chest sweated. Its green plastic lid lay beside the tackle box, upside down and covered in beads of condensation that quivered in the breeze of the electric fan.

Before them lay the remnants of their lunch, unwrapped wax paper littered with crumbs of eaten sandwiches and an open can of Vienna sausages.

"Rain's letting up," Russell said. He cracked open a beer and drank, exposing the stubble on his throat and the sagging collar of his new T–shirt.

The shirt was a present from Clayton. He had purchased it at the new silkscreen shop in the mall. He had gotten the inspiration for the shirt on a school trip the week before at the planetarium, where he watched a galaxy of white stars churn across a high blue dome. Gripping the foam arms of his seat, he had felt as though he might float to the ceiling.

Other fathers at the parish fair had worn shirts that said WORLD'S GREATEST DAD and so forth, and because Clayton hadn't seen his father in so long, he wanted to get him a shirt like that as well. But Clayton wanted to do one better, and he wanted to make his dad proud of him, so he drew a design himself—the sun, stars, Saturn, Mars, and Earth—and above that he printed in solid block letters with shadows: THE #1 DAD OF THE GALAXY. Clayton had to wait a week for them to make the silkscreen from his personal drawing, and when he went down to order a shirt made from the print the store owner asked what size. Clayton pointed to the extra-extra large blank tee pinned on the wall behind the counter. "It's for my Dad," Clayton said. "He's really big."

But the extra-extra large shirt swallowed his dad's torso. It draped over him like a bed sheet. The words seemed deflated, the text sagging so that the shirt read something like H # DD FHE ALXY. Even after his mother had washed the shirt in hot water and dried it all night in the machine, it was still too large. Russell wore it out of love for his child and in defiance of his own overestimated size.

Now, with his scraggly, unshaven face, his scowl, and his blue glasses distorting his eyes, Russell looked defiant. His eyes were yellow and filmy. A navy blue cap rested on the crown of his head, and his patchy brown hair showed through the cap's blue mesh. USS ALABAMA was stitched in gold thread above the bill.

Russell had been sailing for two months and was now on his one-month vacation between voyages. He'd returned home to spend part of that month with his wife and sons.

But shortly after the boys woke up at five o'clock that morning, rain began to come down in sheets. Whitaker was sitting on the back porch tying his tennis shoes when the rain started, and his flat expression eased into a cool smile. Whitaker hated fishing, and he especially hated fishing with his father, so when Whitaker and their mother announced that they were taking the Astrovan to Baton Rouge to catch a matinee and do some shopping, Clayton was not surprised.

The sun broke out by noon, leaving the day wet and refreshed. Clouds drifted off the lake, and under a clear sky Clayton followed his father down to the pier, the loose boards complaining under his father's heavy tread.

Clayton was darker than his father. His face was olive tinted, and he had a long thin nose. His body was long and thin too, and he moved like a blue heron wading through high water. His frame had recently begun to lengthen, as if it had been stretched on a rack overnight, and he felt ridiculous in his gawky body.

Clayton loaded the tackle onto the boat, while his father fired up the Evinrude, the engine gulping heavily at the water, and they shoved off. Clayton went to the bow and looked down into the passing water.

He had once dreamed of hooking a catfish so large that in the sunlight its silver belly shone brighter than the tin roof of the pier shed. He dreamed that he had caught the fish and set a horse's bit in its mouth and laced a leather harness around its flat head. He taught the fish commands and learned to ride it around the lake the way men on television sometimes rode dolphins. Teaching the catfish was easy because it spoke in what he knew to be his dead brother Ferdinand's voice. He had never spoken to his brother, but Clayton knew the voice came from someplace deep in his subconscious.

In the dream he became best friends with the catfish. They lay in the yard for a whole dream day watching clouds drift overhead, but when Clayton looked over, the catfish had died, turned to dry white bones, with his catfish skull fixed and his jaw gaping skyward, so that when Clayton woke up there was a sad loneliness inside of him.

Now, as they made their way over the water, Clayton lay across the Astroturf-covered bow, his arms spread out in front of him like Superman as he pretended to fly past the cypress trees and the occasional open field of grass or cotton or beans, past the houses on the bank, some no more than ragged cabins, others a line of fishing camps, others just rotted trailers, and still others elaborate mansions with lawns as lush and long as football fields.

When the bass boat slowed and the engine quit its high-pitched whining, Clayton pushed off the bow and turned to see his father haloed in sunlight, the shirt flapping on him like a ridiculous sail. His dad looked as though he'd lost a tremendous amount of weight.

Russell scooped into the ice chest and pulled out a Budweiser. He popped the top back with one hand and gripped the wheel with the other. "Get your gear," he said.

Clayton's rod and reel were miniature copies of his father's, and there was no other word to describe them but cute. Clayton had outgrown them. Still, he fetched his rod and reel and took his seat as his father told him how to remove the casting plug and attach the proper hook to the swivel. He pointed out to the shining water and told him where to cast.

"I'll get the crickets for you," he said.

Russell lifted a metal mesh basket from under the console and set it at Clayton's feet. He rummaged around in the chirping mass of crickets—cricket heads, cricket legs, and crickets without heads or legs. His father pinched out a puny-looking cricket and offered it to Clayton. Clayton cringed.

"What's the matter?" Russell said. "Don't be a girl. Grab the shit and run the hook through from here to here."

But Russell did it himself, pushing the hook up through the cricket. Whit had done the same for Clayton dozens of times, but Whit ran the hook from thorax to abdomen, and Russell did it the other way around. The cricket went jittery and tried to squirm out of his father's grasp.

"You want about two feet in your line from the hook to the cork," Russell said, and he took the miniature rod and reel and cast, the red and white cork bobbing a dozen yards from the boat. He reeled until the mechanism clicked, then handed the rod to Clayton.

"You're getting too big for this rig. We'll go to Kmart next week and get you one like mine." He ruffled Clayton's hair, and Clayton smiled.

Russell finished his beer, holding the can underwater until it sank.

"I did that once with a Coke," Clayton said. "Whit and Mom got mad at me."

"No big deal. The can'll make a house for a crab or a fish to live in or something."

"What's it like on the boat?"

"The ship? It's all right."

"What do you do?"

"Hardly anything to do," Russell said. "When I first started going across the Atlantic, I'd go on deck and look at the stars. But I got tired of them so far off. It's like there's nothing but water, and the men on the ship are the only people in the world. You get to hate them because they're always right on top of you. You know what they're going to say before they say it, and you know what you're going to say back before you say it. Mostly I stay in my room."

"I bet I'd like it."

"You don't need to work on no boat. You need to go to school. Don't make the same mistakes I did."

"If you don't like it why do you do it?"

"Quit asking me about the damn boat," Russell said.

Clayton stared at his cork out on the water. He thought about his brother and mother at the mall. Whitaker was sixteen now and almost as tall as their father. He'd told Clayton he thought he was big enough to beat their father up. He said their father was an asshole. Clayton had wanted to tell on Whitaker, but now he decided not to because of how he felt when his father hooked the crickets. Maybe Whitaker was right. Clayton decided he'd rather be at the mall with Whitaker and his mother instead of at the lake with his father.

All afternoon if Clayton's cork went under, Russell let his son reel for just a moment, then grabbed the rod and pulled the fish into the boat where it flopped across the Astroturf deck. With a pair of chrome pliers Russell removed the jutting hooks from the throats of the fish, each catfish pulsing like a gray-blue muscle in the sour-smelling sunlight, each bream or bass or *sac-au-lait* a shifting crescent of gold, green, and silver.

Now the fish they'd caught squirmed in two inches of cold dark river water in the breakaway fiberglass hold. Russell smashed a beer can with his heel and launched it over the bow, wiping the sticky scales and membrane of fish on his shirt. "We don't have our limit yet," he said, opening another beer. "Let's stop at this great spot I know. It's teeming with catfish. It's just down the inlet a ways. Okay?"

Clayton was ready to go home. "Okay," he said.

As the Evinrude hummed low and loud like the engine of an airplane, Clayton rode behind his father on the long bench seat against the starboard gunwale. "Now, you can't tell anybody about this place," Russell said. "It'll just be our secret." Russell steered the boat into an inlet. After awhile he shut off the Evinrude and started the hushed trolling motor, heading quietly toward a double-decked pier.

Clayton stood up to see where they were. The sun was hot on his shoulders and seemed to press against his back.

"Well looky here," Russell said. From the lower deck of the pier music blared from a portable radio, and just out of the shadow of the metal roof two teenaged girls were sunbathing in bikinis. They did not sit up as the boat approached. Their tanned shoulders and thighs shined with oil, and their legs were bent at the knees. Clayton could not stop looking. Looking at the girls felt like reading something that got better and better—the more you read, the more you had to keep reading.

Then Clayton saw that one of the girls was Violet Gidot. He felt embarrassed to see her, but he didn't say anything.

Russell did not seem to recognize Violet. She looked

different from last year. "All the fish are under that pier," Russell said to Clayton. "But I got as much right to be here at this water as anybody else."

Russell took his rod and attached a red plastic worm to the hook. When he cast from the bow, the artificial bait hit the water at the edge of the deck, splashing the girls.

"Jesus!" the blond girl yelled, and both of them raised up on their elbows.

Clayton started to wave to Violet, but when she saw him she shook her head vigorously.

Russell reeled in fast, then bore down on the trolling pedal, sliding the boat a little closer to the pier. He cast again, the plastic worm striking the water farther out from the pier. Clayton saw that his father's eyes were not on the V-wake of the line in the water as he reeled in the lure. His father's eyes were on the girls whose painted red toenails gleamed in the sunlight.

Then Russell flailed the rod and cast wildly. The plastic worm hooked a rubber tire nailed to the edge of the deck. He tugged at the line but the hook only sunk deeper into the tire.

"A little help here?" he said to the girls.

The blond girl shut off the radio and turned to Violet. "What's he wearing? A dress?" She cackled wildly.

Clayton watched his father's face. His jaw clenched, Russell pulled the baggy T–shirt over his head and threw it to the back of the boat where it landed on top of the Evinrude. He took a knife from his pocket and cut the line. "Get my tackle box," he said.

A wave of queasiness washed through Clayton. "I wanna go home, Daddy."

"Do what I tell you, boy."

Clayton scurried to the bench seat and fetched the white plastic box. Russell sorted through the compartments, picking up lures and tossing them aside—a red worm with two hooks, a solid plastic lure with a spinner, and then, from the lone compartment in the bottom of the box he plucked a malicious-looking zebra-striped salt-water jig armed with six hooks and tied it to the end of his line. He wiped the sweat from his brow with his cap. Then he cast, the lure nearly striking the blond girl's hip before it scraped across the planking of the pier and dropped into the water.

"Hey," the girl yelled. "What do you think you're doing?"

"Fishing," Russell shouted. "I got as much a right to fish in any part of the water as anybody else in this parish."

Suddenly an old man stepped from the boathouse at the back of the pier. He was gray-haired and refined-looking, like a priest or an elementary school principal, and Clayton knew that he was Pierre LaFont, the oldest of the LaFonts. He donated money to the parish, to the school, to the church and library. A photograph of him shaking someone's hand appeared in the newspaper almost every week.

"What's going on out here?" LaFont said.

"He tried to hook me," the blond girl said.

"Is that right?" LaFont said. "What're you doing, sir?"

Russell swiftly reeled in the zebra-striped lure. "Fishing," he said.

"You best leave my grandchild be. Just who do you think you are anyway?"

"I've got as much of a right to fish here as anybody. Nobody owns the water!"

The old man looked frail, his plaid pant legs riding high above his scrawny ankles, as he stepped over the girls. "This lake's twenty-two miles long and a mile wide," he said. "Are you telling me you can't find another place to fish? You should be ashamed acting like that in front of that boy there. Get out of here before I call the sheriff. We'll see who owns this water."

The girls stood and wrapped their towels around them. Violet put on a pair of sunglasses and tried to hide her face in her hand. Russell crushed his beer can and hurled it at the pier, but it fell short. He cranked up the Evinrude. The motor churned, then began to make a high-pitched whine. Then it stalled.

"Go on," the old man said. "Get out of here."

Russell's bare chest gleamed in the late sun. Clayton looked from his father to the back of the boat.

"Go check the engine, boy," Russell said.

Clayton climbed over the ladder at the back of the boat and into the water. His father's shirt was mangled in the prop.

"What is it?" Russell said.

For twenty minutes Clayton and Russell chopped the shirt with the knife and pulled the shreds loose with

the pliers. Violet and the LaFonts watched them struggling until finally Russell got the engine started. To
Clayton it felt as if the LaFonts ran more than the town.
They ran the water, and they owned stock in engines and
physics and sheer luck.

"Asshole," the old man said.

Russell hit the throttle, and as the boat swiveled
toward the sun Clayton looked back. The three figures on
the pier shrank away, and from the V-shaped wake scattered pieces of white cloth swirled and spread into the
lake, floating on the water like anonymous trash.

Georgia Pacific Woods 1991

CLAYTON FELL BACKWARDS SNAPPING the crepe myrtle at the edge of his parents' yard. Looking at his shirt, he saw blood. His own. It wasn't terrible. His braces had cut his lip, which had happened all four times he'd boxed. He didn't mean to start boxing.

"What the hell?" Clayton said, looking up at Evan and Whitaker, who both stood over him viewing the damage.

Evan Watts had landed a grazing right hook across Clayton's lip. Clayton had gone wobbly from the blow, then stepped back to avoid a button shot to his chin. Clayton was drunk.

"Shit," Evan said. "Are you all right?"

Evan Watts was a muscular seventeen-year-old, a junior at the Episcopal school in Lafayette. A transfer from East Texas, he had peroxide-blond hair cut in a bowl around his head and no sideburns except for scrapes of pink stubble from the crests of his cauliflower ears to the neck of his shirt. He had a thing for Violet, and so he had invited her and all her friends to ride in the Lafayette parade. In turn Violet had invited him over to Whitaker's house.

The first thing Clayton noticed about Evan was that he stunk of aftershave. He wore it like a GI. Clayton had smelled Evan in the house before he'd even met him—a six-foot stink of Hugo Boss traveled wherever he went. He wore a T–shirt that said BIG JOHNSON with cartoon characters in the shapes of peckers. Clayton hated Evan. He knew from the moment he saw him. He knew in the same way some people fall in love. He hated him because Evan kept putting his hands on Violet's shoulders, or grabbing her wrists when he talked to her.

"Screw you," Clayton said. He rolled his thin frame over and saw the devastated tree. "It's my braces. You didn't cut me."

Laughter rose from the group of older kids on the porch, seniors at Maringouin High School. There was Andrew Lefebre and Jordan Didier, Stacy Pimmeler and Michael Straw. Clayton and Whitaker's parents were in New Orleans visiting friends for the Mardi Gras weekend.

"Take care of your little brother," their mother had told Whitaker from the driver's window of the Astrovan.

Their father was already drinking a tallboy in the passenger seat. "I'm counting on you!"

Clayton had never sparred before this past week, but Whitaker had done it for years, every spring since he was twelve. Boys from the neighborhood squared off in the Bueche's front yard, their bony bodies looking ridiculous in the oversized boxing gloves. Whitaker and Francis. Whitaker and Jason. Jason and George. Whitaker and George. Clayton had watched from the porch since the age of ten. Their mother would not allow her "baby" to do it. He was too young. Maybe next year, she'd always say. Their father had bought the gloves at the Kmart and, out of a tyrannical boredom, forced his eldest son to box boys from the neighborhood. Whitaker hated every minute of it—his father sitting on the front porch, drinking beer and catcalling from the aluminum lawn chair.

"Keep your head down, son! Watch that left! That Cuban kid's fast! Perez, you got a good left, boy! Keep your feet moving, Whit! You'll never kick ass in this life if you don't start now!"

Whitaker told Clayton that he hated the matches, even though he was a decent boxer, dominating Jason and George and Francis. But then he began to throw the matches, slowing his movements, forcing his arms into inertia-ridden leadenness, ducking forward into hooks and jabs until finally he was knocked out by a left hook from the Cuban boy. Humiliated, their father gave up on his dreams of having his older son as a champion, and he turned his optimistic eyes on Clayton.

"Oh no. You're not letting him box, Russell. Not my baby. Forget about it."

And he did forget about it, returning soon enough to the bleary monotony of the oil tankers, coming home each time, less of the man that he was two months before. He sat around the house absently rubbing his fists, massaging the fractures that had healed over after several breaks during his childhood.

But Clayton hadn't forgotten. Just yesterday he'd boxed several friends from school, knocking all of them down viciously in a type of round robin tournament. And tonight he'd challenged Evan to a fight. Gotten drunk for the third time in his life on gin and orange Shasta and pestered Evan to fight until Evan accepted, at which time Clayton was promptly knocked down with one grazing punch.

Whitaker leaned over Clayton, examining him the way a child, hands on knees, will examine an anthill. It was twilight.

"Give me a hand."

Whitaker lifted him from the bushes. Clayton swayed forward upon him.

"You stink of gin."

"Do I?"

"You better not drink any more of Dad's gin. Mom will shit if something happens to you. You're too young to be drinking anyhow."

"I'm all right."

But he wasn't all right. When Whitaker's friends

had arrived in the afternoon, they wouldn't let him drink any beer, so he snuck into the kitchen and poured gin into a plastic squeeze bottle and mixed it with orange Shasta. He sat all afternoon on the pier, drinking under the corrugated tin roof and watching the fish swimming in the sunlit water. The muddy outline of a long garfish darted into the water weeds, moving like a bad thought in the darkness of the pier's shadow. Then there were fish like good thoughts, shimmering minnows darting in netloads below the surface, glimmering and translucent, so that he could see their skeletons, tiny and precise.

On rubbery legs Clayton tried to focus on his opponent.

"You all right, kid?" Evan said. "I didn't mean to fuck you up so bad. Why didn't you tell me he was so young? I thought he was just a scrawny little asshole."

"Shut up," Clayton said. "You're a prick. I wasn't even ready to start."

Evan took a step toward Clayton, but Whitaker came between them.

"Evan, he's drunk. He's just drunk. He's my little brother. I told you to take it easy. You were just supposed to clown around with him."

"I barely grazed his ass. He's the one that was crying to box. He's lucky he's drunk and he's your brother."

Violet came up behind Whitaker. Her hair was cut short in a ginger-blond bob. She wore a black dress that stopped at the ridge of her knees. All the girls were wearing black dresses of similar make and design. She was seventeen now. "Clayton," she said, "you shouldn't be fighting Evan. He's way too big for you."

Violet was still three or four inches taller than Clayton, who was waiting for his growth spurt like people wait for buses. Evan went to the porch and Violet followed him. She shook a beer, then jammed a key into it and set it fizzing at Evan's lips. Evan's hands, still in the gloves, rested on his hips. Whitaker squatted small and anxious in the broken shadow of the crepe myrtle. He turned toward Clayton as Violet fed Evan the beer.

"He's all hot air," Clayton said. "I'd kick his ass."

"You better watch yourself, Clayton. You better not act all crazy tonight. We got to leave soon to get on the float." He held Clayton's shirt in his fist as he talked, clenching it at the collar. He glanced down at the plastic bottle filled with gin and Shasta, which Clayton had been nursing all afternoon. The ice had long since melted, but Clayton had kept on drinking it through the bent straw. Whitaker picked up the bottle and threw it across the hurricane fence into the woods.

"Shit," Clayton said.

The older kids sat on the porch waiting for six o'clock, at which time they would pile into Whitaker's green station wagon and drive to Lafayette to ride in the downtown Mardi Gras parade. But the meantime was filled with drunken chatter on the front porch while Whitaker cleaned out the mowing equipment from the back of the station wagon. Clayton went and sat on the rug in the foyer, listening to the older kids as they drank the beers that Whitaker had kept hidden in the lot by the house. The labels had been bleached off in the sun. No one complained, except Evan, who declared that if he had known all Whitaker had was shit beer he'd have asked his dad to buy them some Mexican gold. Andy Lefebre had the audacity to ask Evan what he meant by Mexican gold.

"Tequila, jackass," Evan said.

Evan's father was a hotshot lawyer whose television commercials ran from Galveston to Gulfport. Everyone had seen the commercials in which Reginald Watts, a sleek blond man who'd been mechanically tanned, opened his arms to the camera in a gesture that could only be taken for complete sincerity and said, "If you've been injured in an offshore accident, you have rights. Call me. Reginald Watts. I know your rights. I am on your side."

"Come on, everybody," Whitaker said. "It's time."

On the ride over, Andrew Lefebre took pity on Clayton, palming him two white pills and pouring into his plastic bottle a quarter of his Jack Daniel's pint. No one noticed. They were too busy sticking their heads out the windows, complaining of the smell of gasoline coming from the back of the station wagon where the lawnmower had been.

Clayton swallowed the pills and sipped whiskey diluted with Mr. Pibb. When they reached the back lot of the Kmart where the floats were parked, Whitaker told everyone to act sober, bored even, so they wouldn't get busted. They did well. Even Evan played the part, yawning when Mrs. Falgoust asked them if they were having fun. She listed their names on a piece of paper and sent them off to float number 42 in a caravan of fifty-four. A big parade by any town's standards.

The Lafayette Mardi Gras floats of the Workers' Krewe were made up mostly of blue-collar workers. Welders, plant men, carpenters, plumbers. Back in the 1950s they walked in the parade each wearing his own working outfit, each man a king for the day, heading down the street with a blowtorch, pipe, hammer, or a ratchet for a scepter. This went on until the 1980s, since which time actual floats were used. Clayton had watched his father walk in the parade and told himself that one day he too would be a plant worker just so he could walk with the workers.

Lafayette floats did not have all the bawdy artistry of New Orleans papier maché. There were no complex caricatured figures worked into the bow and trestle, no mongrel and portly faces of jesters, queens, and mythical animals. Lafayette floats were nothing more than flatbed trailers, nine feet by thirty-five, the rails decorated in plastic strands of purple, green, and yellow, and pulled by a tractor. Each float usually had a theme.

The kids loaded up on float 42, one of the six floats bought on behalf of Texaco for its workers. They had decorated the flatbed with red streamers so that, with the help of a liberal imagination, it looked like a Corvette.

Whitaker was to sit at the front of the float dressed

in the stereotypical old-fashioned driving apparel of goggles, silk scarf, and leather driving gloves. Clayton wore a Texaco jumpsuit and, at the rear of the float, was to lift periodically a 1950s gas nozzle from a fake fuel pump and insert it into the Corvette's tank. Dressed in Texaco suits as well, the other boys milled along the railing like service station attendants. The girls did not wear any costumes except for plastic Mardi Gras masks.

When the tractor pulled them out to Main Street, the crowd roared up to the edge of the float. Beyond the masses the porches of historic houses glowed warmly, and the roofs bled into the black sky. Gray faces, the color of asbestos, blurred by. Children on their parents' shoulders cried out to the riders. And the parents cried out too.

"Hey, mister, over here! Throw my baby something, mister!"

They called the men, the women, the high-school seniors, and even Clayton, mister. And the riders on the floats delivered, tossing yellow string beads and white plastic pearl necklaces and minute pink Frisbees and blazing blue plastic fleurs-de-lis beads out over the railing, where they spun wildly into the crowd.

But from his station at the rear of the float, back by the portable toilet, Clayton drank and watched Evan's every move. Evan had placed himself beside Violet at the rail. Every now and then he touched the back of Violet's low-cut dress, moving into her space to listen to her. In turn she leaned into him as if she could not hear him over the noise.

Clayton lifted the plastic bottle to his mouth, gulping down the syrupy liquor. "Son of a bitch," he said. "Son of a bitch."

Then suddenly Evan pulled away from Violet, stepped past Clayton to the toilet, and ducked behind the black curtain. In a while Violet slinked away from the rail and slipped along the side of the float. She glanced back once at the other riders, then ducked behind the curtain too.

Clayton took a last long swig from the bottle and dropped it to the plywood floor before he stumbled toward the little shed. He thought about yanking back the curtain, but instead he stood beside the stereo equipment, watching the orange geometric lines rise and fall to the tempo of the music, which roared from speakers on the shed roof. All the other riders had clumped at the front of the float, dropping beads into the upraised hands. Whitaker was at the wheel, playing his part. Carefully Clayton pinched back the edge of the curtain.

Violet and Evan were lit from above by a single anemic light. Violet was facing the wall and Evan was sitting, still in his Texaco jumpsuit, his knees on either side of her. He had her dress pulled up above the smooth curve of her hips. Her bare curved buttocks were pale white against the black dress, smooth as milk frozen and carved. Evan's hands moved down the back of her thighs. Clayton wanted to watch them almost more than he wanted them to stop.

Clayton knew Whitaker loved Violet. Some nights when Clayton couldn't sleep he would wander into Whit's room and lie down on the shag carpet. Whitaker would talk about Violet and how it felt to be in love. He spoke of the terrible seriousness of the emotion until Clayton could almost feel it budding inside of him. After listening to Whit, Clayton thought he might be in love with Violet too.

"Don't," Violet said.

"What? You know you like me."

"I do," she said. "This just isn't the place. Besides, what about Whitaker?"

Evan's hand caressed the curve of Violet's hip, his hand moving as if attached to a tiny hinge. "I don't care if he knows."

"I do. You go out first. If they ask tell them I was sick and you were checking on me."

Clayton let the curtain drop and stepped out beneath the passing fluorescent lights of the boulevard. His brother was up from his seat behind the wheel, tossing beads. Clayton flung himself over the railing and dropped on his knees to the asphalt, knocking over two paraders on foot. He stumbled away into the crowd of children, old people, dogs, and bicycles. He pushed through the throngs, and when he was clear of them, ran until the streets were dark and empty, and he found himself alone in the warehouse district. Down an alleyway between two corrugated steel buildings, yellow light poured from high rectangular windows. A briny, sulfurous odor hung in the air, and Clayton went to it.

Down in the pit of the warehouse men wore white aprons stained with blood. A transistor radio on a crate in the corner vibrated with French music while the men labored silently at long stainless steel tables. They pulled catfish from zinc containers of ice and, with electric knives, gutted and filleted the fish and slapped the flesh-colored fillets on sheets of wax paper. Purple and pink guts lay strewn across the floor.

Clayton felt as though he might be sick.

He wandered off to Johnston Street where he hitched a ride from an old black man in an Oldsmobile. The man chain-smoked and preached to Clayton about the merits of being saved. Everlasting life could be Clayton's if only he accepted Jesus Christ as his personal savior. Who would want to live forever, Clayton wondered. Who could begin to want something like that?

The old man let Clayton out south of Maringouin within sight of the house. The single sodium light out in the yard burned, drawing moths, but all the windows were dark. He did not want to go back. He did not want to have to face his brother, or Violet, when they returned. He could not explain to Whitaker why he had left them.

Clayton crossed the highway, heading down a road of crushed clamshell, chalky and pale in the moonlight, and into the woods beyond the Grosse Tete Bayou, beyond where the cane had grown and the Boucodray plantation had stood. He went to the tree house that he and Whitaker had built when they were very young, and there in the darkness he crouched for a long time trying not to cry. But soon Whitaker might come looking for him. And what would Clayton say? What could he tell his brother? How could he explain what he had seen? Clayton went farther into the darkness toward the Georgia Pacific woods.

The Georgia Pacific woods were a swath of pines one mile wide and twenty miles deep that ran parallel to the interstate. As a very young boy Clayton had wandered into the GP woods once at dusk. He knew then that he should have turned toward home. He knew then that he had just an hour of daylight left to trek back down the grass and gravel easement that ran between the Austerlitz and Rougon plantation cane fields. But knowing that he still had gone on deeper into the forest of tall crooked trees.

The company had cut down the straight pines in the 1960s and what remained was a forest of rejects. Corkscrewed trees, trees that grew at queer diagonals, trees that made ninety-degree turns, trees that swirled like spiral staircases to the windy ceiling of the sky. At dusk the light that came across the interstate made the pines seem to sway and shift as if under water and moved by gentle surreal currents.

Now as Clayton reached the GP woods the moon was full and cold and stinging the black sky. He climbed a tall pine whose branches were spaced like the rungs of a ladder, working hand over hand to each sappy branch until the moon became a white portal, fleshy and electric, an end and a beginning, cold and bright.

His legs shook and his chin vibrated as the other bent pines fell away below him. He could feel the wind hushing the earth and his hands covered in sap and the tree swaying in time with the breeze. His entire self clicked into something else. He could feel a ping and a clink deep inside and the sky was darker and raw and untreated. He thought about jumping. He thought about Whitaker and Violet and what people could do to one another. And then he felt like staying up in the tree all night, or longer. Clayton yelled once across the night. When the sound of his voice died out, there was only the sound of the wind through the abandoned trees, a desperate sound over which Clayton knew he had no control.

Pine
1994

C LAYTON SHIFTED IN THE GRASS, squatting against the only tree at the top of the ridge, an awkward loblolly pine. The tree swayed in breezes and bent almost to the crest of the hill when high winds blew the needle rain of the cold season into a slant. Clayton often watched the tree from behind the locked window of his room, wondering if it would snap.

"I don't want to talk about it anymore," he said, dusting pine needles and cobwebs off his jacket.

"Why is that, Clayton?" Doctor Mano said. "You've done so well here. Before you leave I need to know you won't hurt yourself again."

"I didn't mean to hurt myself. I wasn't thinking straight. I know that. Haven't you ever done something stupid? Why don't you ask me something different for once?"

The doctor lay across the grass, a hand propping his bald head. His notebook pages were ultrawhite in the cool sunlight, and his face shone like new wax, eyes small and straining behind the thick lenses of his glasses. Though Clayton had never seen the doctor in anything but inexpensive wool suits of gray and brown, he was wearing ink-dark blue jeans and a college sweatshirt that barely covered his paunch. The doctor looked like a principal on the weekends, uncomfortable in comfortable clothes. He looked down and scribbled in his notebook. His letters were bubbly and symmetrical, the handwriting of an eighth-grade girl.

"Like what?" the doctor said.

"Why don't you ask me what kind of tree I'd be?"

"Why would I ask that?"

"Cause that's what they always ask people in TV interviews."

"Like Barbara Walters?"

"Exactly. Why don't you ask? You could turn loonies out a lot quicker if you'd stop asking how they felt all the time and asked them what kind of tree they would be."

"I don't know that much about trees, I guess." The doctor squinted up at the pine. He tapped his pen at the edge of his notebook. He began to talk about machines again. He used his psychoanalytical language, such as *detachment* and *delusional,* as if he were composing a final draft of an essay on Clayton. As the doctor droned on Clayton stood and looked down the hill at the institution. Cinderblock walls were painted the same muted crème color as the interior. They probably bought the paint in drums, exterior oil and interior latex. The small windows flashed like flint sparks. The place looked abandoned.

"Clayton, are you listening to me?"

Clayton turned his back on the building and faced the doctor who still reclined on the slant of the ridge. Beyond the doctor and down the slope ran a thin wire fence and beyond that was a serpentine asphalt road, which was where Clayton wanted to be. Beyond the road were the woods with sunlight inside the trees. He thought of paper lanterns, of a fire starting in the center of a cane field. He thought of Whitaker.

The wind blew, soft and cool. Pine needles fell around Clayton. He could see how silly he had been. He had believed everything was a machine, which meant nothing was alive and nothing could die, neither him nor anyone nor anything. But his thoughts had gone nasty, and his brain had rusted. The drugs they gave him worked like oil in his head, keeping his mind functioning smoothly. On this day, in his pharmaceutical calm, he could see he'd just had a bad idea, like a nightmare you wake from and see that the dream wasn't so scary after all.

The doctor tapped his pad again.

"I've got to go," Clayton said. "Whitaker's coming today. He's taking me to the baseball game in Baton Rouge."

The doctor stood. "Let's talk about that. Let's talk about that when we get down to the complex."

"You promised me. You promised me if I were cooperative this week you'd let me go. He's coming all the way from New Orleans. You promised. I've only got a week left. It's not my fault you're leaving town today."

"What was the thing you told me about in the cafeteria? What did you want to say?"

"Nothing."

"What was it?"

Clayton looked down at the pine needles. He thought of the many directions they pointed, the many ways to go.

Back in his room Clayton packed his baseball caps, tapes, T–shirts, his two pairs of shoes, one brown leather, one black. When he had signed all the papers and the phone call came through from Doctor Mano, he was given a bottle of the stuff he'd been taking every day for two months. In the smoking room he went around to the guys and shook their hands. Some nodded, some said they'd miss him. Some didn't take their eyes off the television. Robert Marigold looked up from the linoleum for just a moment.

"You'll be back soon enough, Bueche," he said.

When the formalities were done, he walked down the stony drive to the gates. Whitaker's station wagon was parked straight as a ruler on the side of the road. Clayton took a deep breath. He felt a sweet release and thought of the corny image of a dove set free at a football game.

At the gate Whitaker gripped Clayton by the shoulders. "Man, it's great to see you."

"You too."

They drove Highway 17 as the darkness began to bleed into the trees and seep into the ditches. Clayton thought about how the doctors had said the medicine would make him an oak, the medicine would give him roots.

Clayton thumbed through his brother's tape collection, squinting at each case—REM, Johnny Cash, a dozen others. He felt that if he just listened to a perfect song or a perfect album he would not have to worry, he would not end up thinking in circles. He could finally climb out of the dark tunnel into which he'd crawled.

"So, how you feel?"

"I told you. They got me taking these pills."

"Mom and Dad are going to meet us in Lafayette."

"I spoke with them on the phone last night."

"We're going to the Piccadilly. You still like Piccadilly?"

"It's all right."

"Remember when we were kids, and you'd have to eat all your food to see the picture on the bottom of the plate?"

"Sure. The astronaut with his rocket."

"That's right. So what else they gonna make you do?"

"Who? The doctors?"

"Yeah."

"I got to go see a shrink in town every week. And the job. They set it up until school. I'm going to be a baggage handler. I told you that already."

"How's the medicine make you feel?"

"Solid."

"Solid?"

"Plain, I guess."

"Plain?"

"Yeah. I can control myself. I wouldn't trade that feeling for anything at all."

"That's great Clayton. I'm glad you're back."

"Me too."

The roadside was dark now.

"I got to piss," Clayton said.

"All right. We could use some gas anyhow."

Whitaker veered the station wagon into the electric daylight of the gas station, where moths and june bugs skittered across the concrete or whirled at the fluorescent bulbs. Clayton walked into the store while Whitaker pumped the gas. A skinny old woman sat on a stool behind the register, and when Clayton asked her for the bathroom, she handed him a stick wired to a brass key.

Clayton locked the door. The room was painted red, and there were strange smudges on the walls that seemed to constrict when he looked at them. A condom machine hung above the toilet, but in the dim light he could not read the graffiti that covered it.

For a long time he stared at his reflection in the stainless-steel mirror over the sink. His face was a gray shadowed outline. He lifted the toilet cover and knelt. There were voices outside the door, but they drifted away.

He jammed his index finger down his throat and

gagged. His eyes watered. He thrust his finger again, deeper this time, his fingernail scraping the soft palate. Then he vomited. A cold sweat broke out on his forehead, and he seemed to come unhitched from the room as he grabbed the bottle from the sink edge and dumped the pills and flushed. In the mirror his face would not come clear, no matter how close he got to it. He washed his hands and went outside to meet his brother.

Machine Men
in the
Blue Hill Country
1995

WHEN THE RIDGES TURN BLUE AT dusk, the stars blossom against the cool purple dome of the sky, and the snarl of Connor's motorbike rises beyond the pines on Highway 45 and moves across the flatland in front of the house, increasing and increasing until Connor's motorbike rushes into my gravel driveway, and the cycloptic spotlight peers through the window into the dark sanctuary of my bedroom. I am so anxious I bite my bottom lip bloody.

Last night I woke and saw a form in the moonlight. I made out a shape, a person in slack clothes on the floor, before I was truly awake. And it was the same person who is always there. Ferdinand crouched in the corner, his head bowed. The light had fixed him blue. He was like a statue, his nose broken away where I had struck it. His cheeks and eyes had a smooth vagueness, as if he had lain on the ocean floor while oil tanker hulls orbited him, and the waters washed him smooth and featureless.

Outside I step over the welcome mat and the weeds until I reach Connor's bike. The thin plastic frame around his license plate glows red and says NORTH LOUISIANA DIRT BIKE ASSOCIATION. Beneath the metal plate is the word MEMBER. I think, I'm not really a member of anything.

I hitch up my blue jeans to get onto the back of the bike.

"You got anything in your pockets?" Connor says.

"Just your seven dollars."

"Clayton, if you so much as have a goddamn sewing needle, I'll pulverize you."

What can I do? He is my ride to the airport, where the program got me a job as a baggage handler. I got Connor on over Christmas break. Fishing my hands into my pockets, I pull out seven one-dollar bills, a five for coffee and cigarettes, and two scapulas on an elastic brown cord. One is Saint Gabriel, the patron saint of youth, which my mother gave me. The other is Saint Dympna, the patron saint of the mentally ill, which I don't really need, but they gave it to me in Pineville.

"I'm sorry," he says. "I'm sorry, Clayton."

I hand Connor the seven dollars for the week's worth

of rides to work, and he puts the money in his pocket. Like me Connor is five feet eleven inches, but his hair is blond and mine is brown, and his eyes are green and mine are brown, and he is good-looking and I am just regular-looking. We have been living five miles apart for years. We'd seen each other around in high school, but it wasn't until college that we became best friends and dorm mates.

The past few years, I'd been living with my dad near Shreveport. He won't have a television, so when I got to the University of North Louisiana and Conner had a twenty-seven inch JVC television with Surroundsound and a remote, I watched plenty of TV that semester. I pretty much stayed in the dorm room and studied on different books and movies, particularly the ones with stories about androids or robotic men in them, of which there are a zillion. But they all end the same way pretty much.

I attended the university for one semester before I was sent to Pineville. The trip to Pineville was not a grand surprise. When I was seventeen and worked part of one day at Cazayoux's Slaughterhouse, I let all the cows go free out on the corner of Industrial and Seventh.

That day at Cazayoux's my job was to wash the blood slicks off the concrete with a hose. I was supposed to go in between sessions and wash it down—for insurance reasons. I came in with my duck hunting waders on like Mr. Cazayoux told me to. Then I saw the cows lined up in a stainless steel shoot. A conveyor belt moved them toward a fellow with a gun-looking mechanism coiled to a power line. The cows' eyes watched me from over the steel wall. They were asking me to help. But with a plunk and a shudder the first cow fell, and the ground shook. I saw a door latch by the butcher's station and opened it. The cows shot out of there like, well, cows shooting out of a slaughterhouse. It took three hours to herd them. After that Old Mr. Cazayoux with his gray bristly beard under his paper cap predicted where I'd end up. Mr. Cazayoux had one of those electric voice boxes jammed into his fat neck where his vocal cords had been, and a purse full of oxygen with tubes rammed up his nose. In his robot-sounding voice, he told my father, "Russell, one day they gonna ship that boy's ass off to Pineville." And so it was.

I am okay now. I used to think everybody has got machine parts in them. To me people weren't people anymore. They were machines. I used to think that even some animals were machines. Buzzards, if you ever watch them, have abrupt mechanical movements, which are typical for machines, and buzzards are cruel and hateful by nature without even knowing it. But you often can't detect machine men. There are all types of hydraulic systems that can fit into a full-sized machine man, so their movements are smooth and realistic.

But now that I'm on my medicine, I can tell you that there are no machines in people's bodies at all. People are not cold and cruel and heartless. They are

not mechanical and unfeeling, though sometimes at the
airport I wonder. Men and women come and go all day
long, and their baggage comes and goes with them. And
I wonder what's in their bags, and I wonder what's
inside of them, just as I once wondered what was inside
of me.

When we hit the highway the dirt bike snarls like
it's ready to switch over to a higher gear, but there isn't
one for it to switch up to, and that walla-walla-walla
sound comes up from the tires, and the trees bend over
the highway, and the signs to the Lexington Airport flash
by, green and shiny. I hold on tight to Connor.

Let me say this now. I would never hurt anybody.
But Connor has his reasons for asking what I've got in my
pockets.

Connor used to watch porno movies at his parents'
house when his parents were out of town, and sometimes
I would watch them with him. One night we sneaked into
his father's liquor and made some gin and tonics and
sat on the couch in the living room watching a movie on
the TV.

There was one girl that I remember in one of the
movies we watched, and she had two men on top of her.
Suddenly her eyes went soft like a plastic Jesus melt-
ing in a microwave. The men moved like machines,
their hips going up and down like pistons. The movie
was made in 1984, and there was no way I could help
her. What was happening to her had happened long

ago back when I was just a kid. When those men were on top of her I was in the schoolyard back in Maringouin getting picked on by Connor Frommer. There was no way I could help that girl. She was unreachable. And that's when I felt the machine parts begin to work inside me.

When the movie was over and Connor was rewinding it, I went into the kitchen and saw the knife we'd cut the limes with, and I picked it up and took it to the bathroom. I wanted to get to the machine inside of me. I could feel it working, taking me over, and I knew I had to get rid of it.

Connor was the one who called for the ambulance. After the trip to the emergency room and all the bleeding, the doctors made me tell them about everything I'd done that day. What I told them led to my hospitalization. Now sometimes I think about how deep the knife sunk into the soft flesh above my hipbone, and how I couldn't seem to find any steel at all. It is logical, then, for me to think that if—and only if—there were a machine part inside of me and I never found it, then that piece is still inside of me.

So Connor has his reasons. Last week as we rode to the airport I had my hands on his ribs, and I thought I could feel a new, slender piece of steel machine in him. I know this is crazy thinking, but it felt like a curved valve or a piston under his corduroy jacket. The next thing I knew my fingers were picking at his side.

"Goddamn it, Clayton!" he said. "Quit pinching me."

I let go of him. But I took out a small pocket knife and held it, the blade thin and silver and shiny, as the asphalt flashed by beneath us, and Connor turned his head and said, "What the hell?" He spoke so loud I dropped the knife on the highway.

"Connor," I said, "you made me drop my pocket knife."

He pulled over quick on the shoulder and jumped off his bike the way a bull rider jumps off a bull and runs alongside of it. "You son of a bitch!" he said. "You were gonna stab me!" I coasted on top of the dirt bike until I fell into the ditch. He grabbed me by my jacket and shook me. I told him he was acting nuts. I said I was only trying to give him a scare. I told him I would never hurt him, not with a little bitty old pocketknife.

I would never hurt anybody. I wouldn't. And that's what I told Connor, but he was furious, and he rode off and left me there on the shoulder of Highway 19 still three miles from the airport.

When Connor and I get to the airport I punch my time card and take my station, and in three hours I unload and load a 727 out of Memphis, an MD-80 out of Birmingham, and a 737 out of Houston. Out on the tarmac heat shivers off the big engines, and the stink of jet fuel moves across the asphalt like a live thing, and the roar of the turbines after a time begins to rattle me. It happens that way some days.

Over that noise I cannot hear people moving from the airport down the jetway and into the planes, but I know they are there. I can feel them sometimes, and sometimes when I am loading a plane I look up from the conveyor to see them staring down from the windows. When I think of them stepping down the jetway and filing into the shining tubes I remember the cattle in the shoot at Cazayoux's. The people are caught. They are trapped in the machine until they become a part of the machine and the machine becomes a part of them. Yet they rise into the air and go on to their appointed destinations.

During my break I get a to-go cup of coffee from John at the bar and head off to the bathroom. In the stall I check the scar below my abdomen. My flesh is soft and pink like the skin of an infant. There is nothing hard about it at all.

When I come out of the stall door, a businessman is standing at the mirror adjusting his tie. I set my coffee on the counter by the sink, and the businessman considers it, then goes back to studying his reflection in the mirror. He wears blue slacks and a blue jacket and a bright red tie. The creases in his pants are knife-blade sharp. His skin is taut and pink as latex. When he flicks his gaze at me his pupils expand like the lenses on automatic cameras.

"How you doing?" he says. I wait a moment. Water drips in the sink. The only other sound is my breath. I nod at the man to let him know that I know. Then I grab my coffee and hurry out to the terminal.

Back at my station Connor tosses luggage from the baggage cart onto the conveyor that feeds into the baggage check. "Jesus, Clayton," he says. "Why do you do this to me? I'm supposed to be at Gate Seven."

At first all I can think about is the man in the bathroom and the way he looked at me. Then I am sorry I kept Connor waiting. But he is just working here a few weeks, and I am stuck here for as long as I can hold on to this job. "What do you care?" I say. "You aren't gonna be here much longer."

"Don't start, Clayton. Don't start all that."

Connor grips a Samsonite with a leather hand pull and will not take his eyes off me. I get that feeling you get when people stare at you for a long time and you want to hide or cry.

I change the subject. "The other day on the telephone you said you were gonna maybe stop making me pay you to take me to work. Said you'd even give me my twenty-one dollars back for the last three weeks."

He heaves the bag on the belt. "Yeah. I might have said that. But I was kind of drunk when you called. That's twenty-one drunk dollars. The exchange rate on that to sober dollars is about one dollar and a quarter." He smiles and gets back on the baggage cart. "I'll meet you for last break at six-fifteen. All right?"

After awhile all the bags are loaded and gone except

for one silver metallic suitcase that keeps orbiting on the conveyor. It comes through the rubber flaps that hang over the baggage opening and passes by me. For a long time I watch it coming and going, moving around and around.

The businessman sits at the bar. "Barkeep," he says to John, "give me one of those hot dogs." The businessman points a remote control at the television, which is fixed high on the wall in a rigid box of black steel. From the corridor I hear the static voice of the television announcer. His voice is welcoming and conversational.

On the television people are dragged by their feet across the ground. They are dead. Some are naked. A war goes on somewhere far away. Machine men cruise the countryside and slaughter people. Maybe my dad is there, passing by on his steel ship while smoke rises over the mountains.

The businessman looks at me and sneers, then he leans over the bar and says something to John. When the man rotates his finger at his temple John laughs. I turn away and act like I'm looking at a framed poster of a group of ruined marble buildings with weeds growing around them. Beneath it a sharp font reads ROME! In World History at NLU the professor told us that Roman civilization went to pot because lead pipes transported their drinking water, which made them nuts.

I look at the man at the bar, and I know for certain what kind of man he is. He stares at the television and stuffs a hot dog into his mouth. Not once do his eyes blink at the dead on the screen.

The track lights above the bar point in all directions like the lights on a television studio, and the fake mahogany bar shines like the top of a coffin.

Then the man turns to me. "You need something?" he says.

"No," I say.

"No," he says, then he laughs, turning back to the television. "Give me another one of those hot dogs," he tells John.

I do not run. If I ran that would be the end.

When I walk out to meet Connor, a plane sits on the runway. It taxis out, then waits, taxis, and waits.

"You got a cigarette?" Connor says.

"Sure."

Connor lights his cigarette. "I've been thinking," he says. "I sure am sorry about the way I acted."

I don't say anything.

"I know you've been having a rough time with your mom being sick for so long. And what happened last year too. That was real rough."

"Yeah."

"It was rotten of me to leave you there on the highway." He looks off at the plane taxiing for takeoff. "But I think everything's going to be okay with you. You seem better lately. And I'm not just saying that."

Connor pats me on the shoulder the way a brother

would, just as the jet's engines fire and the plane rises, infecting the blue hills, the silvery aluminum convulsing in the sunlight. Then the screeching sound of the plane rolls toward me, the sound of steel on steel, like a freight train stopping fast, a sound that is more terrifying than a human voice crying out.

Grosse Tete Bayou Road 1995

FOR THIRTY-TWO YEARS I, FERDINAND Gidot, walked this road with Henri, Johny, and Baptiste. Every morning at five we would say the rosary along with that skull-faced Bishop O'Mally on Channel Four, and when it was still a chill in the air, we would take to the crossroads of Highway 19 and the Bayou Road. We were up so early the doves didn't start flying over the sugarcane in Riche's field till we were two miles down the road.

I'd always walked that road alone in the mornings to let the cattle out to graze that back piece of property I got between Riche's cane fields. But the day after Melise passed away, Henri come to walk with me. He knew my routine and wanted to watch over me, I guess. Thirty-two years ago. Then Johny come along one morning, then

Baptiste, and it was all of us for all them years. It's a good mile and a half and it's good for the health. That's what we told people when they asked us why we walked. People always gotta have a sound reason for things like old men walking so far.

For a time when I walked I'd milk the three cows that stay in the barn. But it got to where milking every day took too much out of me, so now the Gonsilan boy milks. But he called at five-thirty this morning and said he was sick and asked if I could do it. So that's what I'm to do.

One morning in 1986 Baptiste didn't show. He had passed on in his bed the night before. At his funeral Baptiste looked like a wax figure in that big shiny coffin. He was smiling, but if you knew his smile you could tell it wasn't his at all but just a smile worked on with fingers and makeup. Only Baptiste himself knew which face muscles to work when he smiled. And I guess there is a combination lock to the heart that works that, and when the heart stops, the smiles quit coming.

Henri passed away in that cypress cattle barn of his. Sue found him sideways in the hay. He'd gone out to feed those two black skittish head of his.

And two weeks ago Johny was walking with me, and he started out just fine, but when we got to that green oak before Riche's field he was hunching forward, so I said, "Johny, quoi c'est ca? Virer de bord?"

And he said, "Non. I'm fine, Ferdinand. I got a raler. It's all right."

So we went a ways until it was like he was going to fall over. He was breathing heavy. I told him to stay there by the oak tree and I'd go get a car, but when I come back, he'd made it all the way to the Bayou Road sign. His face was gray, gray, gray.

His son Louis took him to the hospital. They said he had a problem with his equilibrium, that was all, but the doctors found a tumor the next Tuesday and he passed on Wednesday. Aneurysm.

Now it's just me. This is the third day I'm walking since Johny's funeral. If Melise was here she'd tell me not to. Tell me to stay home with her and drink coffee and watch the sunrise from the kitchen window. But Melise passed on from the cancer and has been gone all those years. So it's like the old-timers say, *Le jour est apres se faire!* and I walk alone.

From where I stand by the highway the cattle barn is just a distant brown speck of wood. The road before me is crushed shell that Riche drops in the ruts, and it runs from the highway along my house all the way back to that property I got with the crawfish ponds and the bayou swooping around, yeah.

It's strange how them engineers built up the highway so it wouldn't flood, and the road falls in front of you steep. Going down, all of us except for Henri would hold to each other's elbows. A small descent can tempt a fall. But Henri had the big head his whole life, so when it come to walking down, he would sidestep all by his lonesome.

187 All Saints' Day

I'd say, "Mais, Henri, you a real cowboy, you!"

We'd all laugh. Henri would laugh too. "I don't want no help walking," he'd say. "But if I hit that ground y'all better come on!"

But he never fell, and each time when he made it down himself he had that gambler's grin. Going his own way gave him fuel for the rest of the walk, I guess. But now I think these days when I'm out on the road how it's the little things, like walking hills, that slow you down. As you get older there's a lot of little things you never thought on before, more than you'd ever figured on thinking about—hills, ditches, bayous—a lot of obstacles.

The bayou is brown and low and runs into the river lake. If you asked me its color I'd tell you mud, and out on that water the turtles get up on the cypress stumps together. I always get a kick out of them turtles. It's no fun to be alone, not even for the turtles, you know?

When I look out at the country along the bayou where everything is trees and sky and road, I think about what Baptiste said the first season we walked together.

He said, "South Louisiana doesn't have any scenic elevations to it."

"How you mean?" Johny said.

But I knew how Baptiste meant. I had done my piece in Europe and seen from different elevations. Johny had that bad ear and didn't go into the service, and probably had never been further than Texas. But Baptiste was always saying things that made me think. Johny figured thinking on things would ruin his walk. I figure thinking about things is good for a walk—gives it a plot and destination.

"I worked for the company in Colorado for six months back there," Baptiste said. "There was always different elevations. So you could tell where you were at and where you been. It was real nice to look off at another place."

"What good that do you to look off at another place?" Johny said.

"People in Louisiana don't have no place to look off to," Baptiste said. "So they looking at each other. They look too hard and what they see rests heavy on their minds. It do us all some good to be able to look off this place. Give a man a way of thinking outside of where he is. Free him up. A man can't get freed when all he sees is a ditch or a bayou or sugar cane blocking out the sky."

"Or an ugly face like mine!" Henri said. Which made us laugh. Henri didn't say much, but when he did, you had a good laugh.

When I get to those tiny willows and oaks there, I know I am halfway to the barn. Johny and me planted the willows. Seventeen years ago, Johny said, "Ferd, it sure would be nice if there was a patch of willows or oaks here for us to rest under."

I told him, "Johny, it'd take ten years for them trees to bring shade. There's no point in us planting now. We won't be able to go walking in ten years, I don't guess."

Seventeen years ago. It was just last year that we

said how we was foolish not to have planted them trees back then. How we figured too small of ourselves.

Johny said, "I been figuring too small of myself my whole life, I guess. And it's a trickster's way that I'm only figuring that now."

So him and me planted those little trees one year ago.

I walk up to the trees and put my hands under the branches. My joints are swollen and my veins look like they gonna bust, but the green leaves of the little branches is wide enough to shade my hands from the sun for a moment while I stand there looking down to the bayou.

It's a funny thing how so much gone by, how old I got. I figured when I was young that old people's spirits got old with their bodies. I always thought that cause it just seemed like logic. That's the hardest part about it, how my spirit seems to still be a boy's spirit. How it wants to keep going, and it don't want to understand how things are. I am eighty-one years old. The oldest one at the funeral home last week.

I seen those young girls at Mass that look like Melise used to look. I can appreciate it now how you can love them. When you're young, you figure it's only cause of the physical that you feel like that. But now my physical just about quit, and I can see it's the spirit of me that admires girls. I see all that possibility in their eyes and the way their faces look when they turn their heads to pass the basket down the aisles. It's a good thing to see. You get to understand the seeing of it is just as nice as the physical. But maybe that's just me. As for Johny, I almost expected him to climb out of the coffin when that Distefano girl walked by.

The doctor tells me I shouldn't want to walk so much anymore, says I should rest. This morning I felt a hardness in my bones like they was saying, "Ferd, I had enough. I done plenty for you. Now you let me be." But I don't mind my bones. It hurts to do the walking, sure, but I figure I'll just keep on till my nickel runs out.

Sometimes I walk and think about my grand-children, how they have no time for me and how one hundred dollars won't do it for them no more. I recall when one hundred dollars was a fortune and all we had was time on us. Time sat on my shoulder like a fat quail. It's a thin finch now. It's a *'ti pap*, you know?

I open the gate latch and walk toward the barn, and I can hear those cows moaning. I think of their teats sagging almost to the dust, full of all that hot milk. I think of all that wanting sound they make when they hear me coming up to the barn, but I go on past the barn anyway. They can wait.

Past the barn a quarter mile the road goes from dirt to asphalt and the new development starts. Riche must have got a pretty piece for that property. But already spent it all for sure. That's how those Riches always been. He's driving an old pickup one day, sells his acres to them developers, and the next day he don't probably have one dime more in his bank account, but he's driving him a Cadillac to the casinos.

Those workmen with their bulldozers don't come here till six-thirty. I seen those yellow engines waiting for the men, sitting ready in Riche's field. I guess it was bound to come when they built up that highway extension.

When we was children, the circus would come to Maringouin. We would pay a nickel and see the clowns and the musclemen with the handlebar mustaches and the pretty ladies in silver tights up on the high wire. Once, after everyone went home, I hid under the bleachers and listened to the trapeze ladies talk their funny Yankee talk while they smoked cigarettes. Finally one of the women heard me giggling and chased me out of the big orange tent. That's the feel I got now. My nickel had run out and I'm still under the tent fly.

When I get to the asphalt road I feel the wind, and it says, "Old man, you so hunkered down, you lucky I don't decide to blow you over!" I see the clean new concrete curbs and imagine all the new houses with those new people living inside of them. They won't know that this was our piece of country and we minded it until everything changed.

I got to rest. I turn back around to the barn, and when I do I go down to my knees and the blackness of the asphalt is wet and cool on my hands. I see doves lighting on the cypress trees. They always watch you like they want to say something but don't have the tongue for it. Sometimes you wish they did. What would they say if they could?

The sun is up a good ways over Riche's field where all that new black dirt is ready for a new house, for a young family to set up in it, and the sky glints like those circus women's costumes. I can almost see my own self when I was nineteen years old, before I worked at the sugar mill and scarred my hands. I can almost see this boy in a pressed white suit with a yellow carnation in his lapel. He's walking past me down that wet asphalt road, and he's heading toward a pretty girl with her hair cut in a bob like Melise used to wear. My *grand coeur* fills up.

Then the boy is gone and I am very cold. A few cattle stomp across the field, stirring dust, while the cows in the barn moan, their teats swollen. The doves settle down on the road in front of me. I've shot doves, so many you'd think they'd stay clear. But that's the sad Jesus way to a dove, a creature most unlike a man. A dove wants to be close and quiet. I lay on the cool asphalt and taste dust, and the doves hop close, almost onto my hands. A moaning rises over the fields. I lift my head to listen and the doves fly away, the wing-stirred air touching my face. I watch the doves lift over the distant cane, and I stand to follow them.

The Last Cane Harvest 1996

WHITAKER WALKED ACROSS THE cane fields where fires he had lit still burned and climbed into the company truck. The night was starless. The fields reeked of kerosene and sucrose, which he could taste in the back of his throat. He had heard that the farmers would stop burning this season. Every year this rumor made its way through the sugar mills and the fields and the tack sheds. The government wouldn't allow fires anymore, but every year they burned, breaking down the cane so it could be hauled in trucks to the local mill where it was ground and processed into syrup. When the billowing smoke shifted in the wind, Whit could see the clouds lit by the fires. He started the truck. He was tired of sugarcane. Tired of fire. Every parish was a smoldering netherworld of smoke and flame. He wanted to see mountains.

He had given up his job working at the front desk of a hotel in Maringouin. One night a young salesman named Vincent from Nashville had brought to the desk a bottle of whiskey and shared it with Whit.

"You mean you've never left the state?" Vincent said. "You've never seen mountains or snow?" Whitaker said he hadn't, and Vincent told him about the different mountain ranges, and these tales put into Whit's head a blurry desire to leave the sunken lowlands where he'd always been.

But here he was—still in these lowlands where oaks grew monstrous in the flat fields, though now in the puny light of the truck's headlamps the trees seemed like black paper silhouettes. As he drove down the lane, Whitaker could see the horizon across the highway in fields he'd burned last week. There the sky was a layer of bruised purple over the charred earth.

Whit had told the other men who set the fires that he would light the last field, so they had gone down the road to a lounge on the highway. He said he would be along shortly, but now Whit pulled up beside the trailer, the makeshift office where Violet worked and slept. The men who set the fires with Whit shared a single motel room, one of them always taking a shift of sleep on the stale carpet. Violet had the trailer to herself.

The truck headlamps lit the trailer, creating a silverish white trace around it. The trailer was stained with cane ash on the front side and black ash stuck to the windows where the shifting winds had packed it. Whit killed the engine and the lights and got out, waiting for a long while outside the door. Finally he rubbed at the window with his elbow and the cane soot fell away like black snow. Inside Violet stood by a heater vent, waving her hands in front of it as if to dry them. She was trying to keep warm. On the small card table was an adding machine and a Steen's syrup can, which Violet used for an ashtray. Whit tasted his fingers, which were sweet and bitter with raw sugar, then turned around and saw the wind cutting smoke across the way he'd come, blacking out the road. He spat twice and swung open the trailer door.

"Shit," she said. "You scared the shit out of me." He could tell by the casual way she said the word that it had drifted into her everyday speech. This made him feel sad.

"I'm sorry," he said. In the past few years small wrinkles had formed at the corners of her eyes, and her irises were black as slick stones. Her hair was a bit greasy and pulled back in a bun. The oatmeal-colored sweater she wore was tattered and had a cigarette burn through one sleeve where ash had fallen. She was beautiful. Whitaker felt that only he could see her beauty, which made him feel sad and fortunate at the same time.

Now it was the end of November, and the cane was burning. Violet had taken this job with the Dixie Crystal Company, traveling from field to field, keeping books on the loads and taking checks from the local mills. Her friend Milly LaFont had gotten the work for her. Milly had gone to college to start her junior year and asked her grandfather—Mr. Pierre LaFont—to give Violet a job. Whitaker had worked the entire burning season just to be close to Violet.

She had finally broken it off with that jarhead back home. Evan Watts. He'd joined the police academy. When they rode in the truck, Violet would tell him about Evan again and again, then when she finished talking she would look off at the anonymous green lines of cane that flickered past like frames in a movie reel. Whitaker tried to ignore the things Violet told him. He didn't want to think about her with anyone else. This was his chance to take her away.

"What do you want?" she said.

"I need to tell you something."

She tapped a cigarette three times against the pack. "I thought we weren't going to make this difficult," she said.

Her face was thin, pale. He could see the delicate outline of her skull as she lit the cigarette and took a long drag.

He palmed a small box from his pants pocket. His fingertips, stained with soot, blended with the black velvet cover. He'd bought the ring in New Iberia, and now he was broke. "I've thought about it. You make me feel like myself. All this life everybody's seemed dead to me. I'm becoming one of them. I work and I cough, and I grind my teeth all night." He curled his lips like a horse, but she turned and took another long drag, blowing smoke at the ceiling, where it roiled and spread. "If I let you get away I'll have nothing."

"What?" she said.

He took a step toward her, and she took a step back. The windows were black, and the electric light seemed all that more vital in the small room. The heat clicked on, blowing dry against the back of his neck.

For the past month he had practiced a speech as he worked the fields, talking to himself as he slung kerosene and lit fires in measured distances before the reapers and the tractors came. Now his words slipped away from him, and he looked around the room trying to catch his breath. Empty cigarette packs, Moon Pie wrappers, and load receipts cluttered the corners.

"I've been searching," he said.

She shook her head.

He was making a fool of himself, and he couldn't help it. "You're the one," he said.

He moved toward her across what seemed to be a vast expanse, then popped open the box and in one motion took her hand and tried to slide the thin gold ring up her finger. But the burning cigarette was pinched between her pinky and ring finger, a European affectation she had picked up from Milly LaFont who spent her summers in Tuscany.

That night he and Violet were together, and it felt to Whit as if they were conceiving a world. Afterward he got up to wet some rags Violet kept in the sink, and he stuffed them under the threshold to keep out the black gasps of smoke that came when the wind shifted. Then, shivering, they wrapped themselves in a single ragged sheet and huddled under the heater vent. They made plans. They would harvest one more year and take the money and buy a house in Florida. They would get out of Louisiana. They would have a son and name him Ferdinand.

When Whitaker woke the windows were caked black with soot. Only a small yellow swatch of sunlight came in at the edge of a pane, staining the toes of his mud-caked boots. He rubbed his stiff neck. She was not beside him. She had taken to the couch, two lint-matted blankets wrapped around her.

"Violet," he said. "Vi-o-let." A grin bloomed on her face, and she rolled over and said a name he didn't recognize. Never mind, he said to himself, never mind. This was a new day, a new life, and yet suddenly he felt as though he'd done something wrong. Everything he'd done before now had been screwed up and delusional. He went and sat on the edge of the cot, taking care not to frighten her.

"Hey," he said. "Let's go get some breakfast."

She didn't stir. She was breathing heavily, almost snoring, and in the gray light of the trailer he could make out a few small chicken pox scars marring the smooth flesh of her cheek. He had not noticed them before. He pushed a stray lock of hair behind her ears and saw again the soot on his hands.

He wrote her a note on a grimy accounting sheet that said he was going to the Waffle House down the highway and that he would bring her back a pancake and egg breakfast. *I love you!* he wrote. He added a heart to his signature. Then he crumpled the sheet and tossed it on the floor. He wrote her another note that said, *Went for eggs*.

Outside he was taken aback by how blue and clear and perfect the sky looked. A thresher had come in the early hours and cut the tall singed cane, and for the first time lush woods were visible in the distance. "How about that," he said, looking off toward the woods. "Something new." He pissed in the tall blackened weeds grown up behind the trailer, and steam rose from the cold ground. Zipping his fly he took a few steps back from the trailer and shook his head.

The white metal walls and the roof were crusted in black soot as if the whole place had caught fire. He smeared his fist and forearm across the glass, and soot came down in chunks and a little light fell into the room where Violet slept. He told himself he was finally happy.

Whit cut through the woods toward the highway. Towering oaks and pecans pressed against the sky, and the air was chilled and damp, and it tasted of wet wood and leaves. The rising sun dappled the ground, which was littered with pecans that were too green to eat.

By the time he got to the Waffle House the traffic was heavy on the highway and the sun was well into the sky. He walked in and gave his order at the counter and waited, watching the fry cooks until someone tapped his shoulder. The company superintendent. "How ya doing?" he said.

Whit nodded.

"We had a good work here," the superintendent said. "You did a good job. I'll pass the word to the managers. Pass your name along, I mean." The man seemed a little drunk. He had been out all night celebrating the harvest.

"Oh," Whit said. "Thanks."

"You come to meet them?" the superintendent said.

"Who?"

"Louis and Bill. I saw them in here a little bit ago. They said they were looking for you."

"Oh," Whit said. "Yeah. Sure."

"It's a long trip to the next field. You all best get on the highway before the Thanksgiving traffic. That's the worst. All those families getting home."

"Right," Whit said. "Sure."

They shook hands and the superintendent headed out the door.

Whit took a seat at the counter and looked over to three red vinyl booths along the far window. In the corner a man in a dark jacket and tie sat alone, reading a copy of the *Houston Chronicle*. In the middle booth sat another man, thirty years old or so, just a little older than Whit. The man wore a plant worker's jumpsuit, and beside his grease-smeared plate lay welder's goggles and a grimy cap with a pattern of alligators on it. To Whit's surprise the man was reading a novel. In the last booth was a family, two young boys with their parents. The father wore a Donald Duck tie. He had the paunchy swollen look—like a floating cadaver—that all married men had. The mother had been pretty, but now there were dark circles under her eyes, and the youthful outline of her face had been worn down with worry and fatigue.

They both possessed a great reserve as they dealt with their children. The boys were kinetic little skeletons with bowl haircuts. They pressed their hands to the glass above the booth, streaking the window with grease. They spilled salt from the shaker. They knocked over their Cokes. They laughed and slapped the booth seats. They dropped forkfuls of egg on the table. Each incident aroused only sedate concern from the parents, while the men at the other booths looked up nervously at each fallen spoon or spilled glass.

When Whit's order had been spatulaed into Styrofoam boxes and bagged, the family rose from their table, the parents corraling the children outside. Whit held the door for them.

"Appreciate that, buddy," the father said. "Hey, you need a ride somewhere? I saw you walk up. You don't want your food to get cold."

The offer surprised Whit. A ride from a family of four was as unlikely as a trip in a limousine.

"I appreciate that," Whit said.

"Well, come on," the man said.

They loaded into a minivan strewn with suburban paraphernalia—video cassettes, cereal boxes, smashed sandwiches, bits of orange peel and dried cheese, pulverized Cheerios, receipts from Toys R' Us. Everything was ripped or crimped or broken.

The wife did not seem to notice or care that Whit was with them. She leaned her seat back and closed her eyes.

"Where you from?" the man said. Whit sat at attention in the middle of the van. Behind him the boys squealed and wrestled and waved at passing cars.

"Maringouin," Whit said.

"Well, howdy doody. That's where I'm from."

"No kidding," Whit said.

"Sure am. Howdy doody!"

Howdy doody? Whit thought. The man must have picked up the exclamation as a parent, a replacement for a less wholesome expression such as *no shit*.

"Are you a Blanchard?" the man said. "You look like a Blanchard."

"No. I'm not."

"You look the spitting image of Dale Blanchard's son. He leads that Christian youth organization."

"My dad's Bueche," Whit said. "Russell Bueche."

"Oh," the man said. "Yes, I know him." Then he was quiet.

"Where are you all headed?" Whit said.

"Maringouin actually. Live in Lake Charles. But my

nephew's getting married. We're going to the engagement party. Dominic Shinier. You know him?"

Whitaker did know Dom. He was a good guy, a white hat at one of the plants. He always wore a tie with his short-sleeve shirts. "Yeah," Whit said. "Who's he marrying?"

"Milly LaFont."

"No kidding?"

"Yep."

"That's an odd pair. I mean, two different personalities."

"It's a sudden thing. She's due."

"Oh," Whit said. He looked out the window. The trailer passed by. "That's my stop back there at that trailer."

The man pulled off on the shoulder. Trucks roared by, scattering cane husks across the asphalt.

"Say, you don't need to go on any farther do you? I'd let you ride if you are. I don't mind. I could use the company. My wife's zonked out. She didn't sleep a wink last night. She worries about the boys."

Whit looked at the woman in the front seat. She was breathing heavily, her face slack. He thought of the ride, of him and Violet crammed between the children and the parents. The notion was unbearable.

"I don't know where I'm going, really," Whit said. "But thanks."

As the minivan pulled away, Whit stood at the side of the highway. He thought of Violet there in the squalor of the trailer. He did not doubt that she was still asleep. He tossed the plastic bag of food in a clump of charred weeds and started up the highway.

The ditches were littered with cane stalks fallen from the grates of passing trucks, and the billboards at the edges of the fields sagged. He looked back at the trailer, wanting Violet at any moment to step out the door, but she did not. The door remained shut. That meant something. It was a sign. The farther down the highway he walked the more the trailer resembled nothing but a brick of charcoal.

An eighteen-wheeler was stopped on the shoulder ahead of him. The driver locked up his trailer and wiped his hands on a brown rag. He was older than Whit, bearded, a tall thin man with red cheeks.

"Where you headed?" Whit called to him.

"Knoxville."

"Need company?"

"Sure, climb in."

Whitaker got in the truck. In the side mirror he could see the reflection of the trailer, a dab of tar on the horizon. He felt like a coward.

The truck rolled east on Interstate 10, and by dusk they were on 65, the hills of Northern Alabama rising on either side of the cab. The driver had a bottle of bourbon, which he shared with Whit. At first the bourbon stung his gut, then after a while it felt right to be on the cold highway at dusk. Finally Whit slept.

He woke alone in the cab to mountains skirted in fog and snow falling and small white drifts forming at the edge of a truck-stop parking lot. The snow came down hard, and the cab shook, the diesel engine straining to stay warm. Whitaker watched the snow as it began to cover the asphalt, burying cans and plastic bottles and paper cups strewn across the lot. When the snow finished falling no one would see the trash, but Whitaker knew it would still be there.

Concierge 1996

WHITAKER WAS A DESK CLERK, BUT HE referred to himself as "the concierge." Though most of the guests called him "the guy behind the desk" or "the desk clerk," a few long-term renters, mostly salesmen, would phone from their rooms and ask "the concierge" for favors. Whitaker would hurry down the road to the fast food restaurant and fetch burgers and fries, or stop off at the corner gas station to buy toothbrushes, combs, magazines, pints and half pints of Jack Daniel's, Jim Beam, or Taaka, or sometimes even a one-pound satchel of over-salted boiled crawfish.

But this Saturday night was quiet. None of the familiar salesmen were in because the gentlemen's club down Highway 41 was open until two A.M. and, for one night only, it featured a special act—one "Miss Quick Draw" out of Abilene, Texas. "Miss Quick Draw" wore only a cowboy hat, boots, and a belt. She roped men, and sometimes women, up to the stage, or so the salesmen who had caught her act in other venues told Whitaker. Whitaker wanted to see what the women in the club looked like. He was resigned to the notion that a gentlemen's club was the place men went when they wanted to be with women. To be with them in any other way required an intimacy that was as elusive as a winning lottery ticket.

He had stayed in Tennessee for more than a month and returned on a Greyhound, arriving in Maringouin in the middle of the night. The next morning he had begged the general manager of the hotel to let him on again. Whitaker had had to start over, though, working the night shift.

Whitaker looked past his reflection in the glass doors of the foyer and out into the dark parking lot. Cars flitted by, carrying people to somewhere else. If the passersby were to glance at the structure in which Whitaker worked, they would not think of the building as a hotel, but instead they would see it as nothing more than a shabby motel.

The box-shaped hotel squatted to the east of an overpass where two highways criss-crossed. It was built of wood and covered in faded pink stucco that was cracking in places, baked by the sun. At night, when Whit ran errands for the guests, he would walk past two breakfast restaurants near the overpass, and sometimes he would pause in front of the gas station where there was a large empty cage. A tiger had been kept there for years, a tourist trap, a trick to get people to stop and buy gas and

Twinkies and plastic junk. Whit would stand in front of the cage, its rusting gate swung open, while car head-lights swept across a crude painting on plywood of a growling tiger. The cage still smelled faintly of cat—a pungent urinary stink that was stronger after a rain. When he turned from the cage, he could see the motel—a dis-embodied organ with lights in the windows going on and off like electric pulses across synapses of pinkish tissue.

Indeed, to Whitaker the motel was less of a building and more of an organ, folded tissue inside of which peo-ple lived, slept, ate, made love. The life of the organ went on and on, twenty-four hours a day, people coming and going like sustaining blood from dim, stale chambers. At night Whitaker often wandered the hallways, the arteries of the hotel, which were bathed in a strange greenish light. As he wandered he envisioned the people on the other side of the doors. In one room a lonely businessman sulked, in another an infant cried, in another a woman shouted at someone on the other end of a phone line. And maybe in some room a man entered a woman for the first time, swimming in vividness, a triumphant flood. The man held the woman for a long time before he moved on to other places and other women, but he would recall that moment in the motel room for the rest of his life. Some-times the man would draw upon it for sustenance. He would bleed it for endless miserable days.

When Whitaker first started at the motel, he would go into the rooms after the cleaning women were finished. The rooms had the anonymity of tombstones, and, like tombstones, the rooms could not tell of the complexities of lives that had been there. So, from the hallways and behind the desk, Whit preferred to live his life. He was obsessed with hallways, he was a champion of corridors. A hallway was preliminary to emotion. From a hallway one departed or arrived, and the strange green light lent to each imagined event the sadness of life's in-between moments.

Whitaker stepped up to the glass doors and opened them, damp heat pouring into the cool foyer like smoke. The hot air seemed to want to retreat into the cold air-conditioned room, but the room only grew hotter. It was a kind of failure.

This evening the blue-suited salesmen had come and gone. There were two kinds of salesmen: handsome bastards and poor pitiful bastards. The handsome bastards wore horn-rimmed glasses and Armani suits. They stepped to the desk as if Whit were nothing more than a cigarette machine. They ran their fingers through their gelled hair or spoke over their shoulders to a colleague. They were obnoxious, yet Whit tried to project an air of sophistication in hopes they would ask him to go out for a cocktail sometime. They worked for petrochemical plants or else sold to the plants, peddling pipes or valves that would make sizable profits for anonymous executives. Sometimes he thought of telling the handsome bastards that this job was only a temporary one and that as soon as he had enough money saved he intended to go to the University of New Orleans and major in engineering.

Whitaker leaned against the open door, watching insects swirling beneath the lamps of the parking lot. A june bug fell at his feet and struggled along on its back. Whit kicked it away, and it righted itself and flew. He thought about one handsome bastard in a pinstriped suit. He had smelled like plastic. He had not spoken a single word but had tipped Whitaker with a hundred dollar bill, sliding it from the inside pocket of his pressed jacket. Everything about the man seemed pressed in a machine, crisp and smug. Even Ben Franklin seemed to sneer at Whitaker as he took the bill.

But the poor suffering bastards, they would talk to him. Sometimes they wouldn't leave him alone. The poor suffering bastards could relate to Whit, which he hated them for. His father had been one of them for awhile, a valve salesman out of Shreveport before he failed at that and returned to the plants. So every time Whitaker spoke to the poor suffering bastards he was reminded of his father. Their words stank of cheap coffee. Their eyes were yellow with disappointment, and their stomachs were bloated as if they were rotting from the inside. They wore the same fake leather shoes his father had worn. Exhaust hovered over their cars. They were the ones who came to him, defeated, the best of them shilling aluminum siding and the worst pushing steak knives.

But on a Saturday night the handsome bastards and the poor suffering bastards were all in it together down at the gentleman's club. They were one and the same.

While Whit held the door open, in walked Charlie 217. An insulation salesman from Alexandria, he had been staying in room 217 for three weeks. Charlie 217 was a perfect example of a poor suffering bastard.

"Hey, concierge."

"Hey, Mr. Charlie."

"How's the fort?"

"Okay"

"The girls, I tell you, Whit, the girls they have down there. You been yet?"

"Nope."

"Next time, Whit. Next time I'm taking you down. We'll get you a private show, Whit. They've got the private rooms. How'd you like that?"

"Sure. Sure."

Charlie 217 stumbled to the coffee pot on a low table in a corner and poured himself a cup. He caught his visage in the hallway picture—a commemoration of the World's Fair of 1984 in New Orleans. He tucked in his shirttail and grinned at the reflection as if he were smiling for a photograph. "Handsome devil," he said, and he clicked his tongue. He laughed and turned to Whit, who had settled back behind his desk. "Any traffic tonight? Any girls come through?"

"Yeah, a couple," Whit said, which was a lie.

"Oh, yeah? How bout that. Old Whit was working 'em over, and I'm staring up at em like they're in a glass box."

"I had to call the cops on them."

"Don't say it, Whit. No, don't tell me that."

Whitaker gazed down at the man's gold wedding ring. "Yep."

"Next time you see something going on around here, don't dial 911. Dial 217, and old Charlie'll handle the situation."

"Sure."

"Tell me about them, Whit. Tell me the score."

Whit told Charlie just what he thought Charlie wanted to hear.

Most of Whit's stories came from Mr. Glass, a sniveling old concierge who'd worked in a New Orleans hotel and had befriended Whitaker. Glass boasted of his ability to sit for hours and watch people without ever moving a muscle. Mr. Glass had a wealth of stories because, he said, at the hotel in New Orleans he had constructed a catwalk of two-by-twelves running above the top-story suites. Mr. Glass said he had drilled small holes in the ceiling and screwed in peephole magnifiers so that, on his knees, he could view the entire room through the fisheye lens of the peephole. He told Whitaker he could see everyone and everything in every corner of the room through the rounded fisheye glass. This made Whitaker think of God looking down on Earth, waiting for the people to do something or not do something.

Salesmen loved the stories. Even traveling preachers liked them. Whit wondered if those obsessed with fighting sin couldn't help but be obsessed with sin itself. He always gave them stories when they asked, and sometimes when they didn't, often changing the details a bit, the better to gauge each listener's reaction. The salesmen or the preachers would move in close, elbows on the desk, and become silent.

Charlie casually leaned one elbow on the desk.

"Two young girls," Whitaker said.

"Young? How young? Seventeen? Eighteen?"

"Eighteen. I think."

Charlie closed his eyes. "In what?"

"Tight skirts, awful tight, and silvery shirts, you know the ones. One girl was a peroxide blond, and skinny, the other was a brunette, a little taller, and much better built than the other one."

"How'd you figure them?"

"It wasn't so hard, the way guys were drifting in and out of room 122 every thirty minutes or so. Like a factory. Three or four guys at a time."

"All white boys?"

"Pretty much. Three or four at a time."

"Unbelievable."

Whitaker gave so many details he began to think he'd actually witnessed the event. He said the red light on one police car was out, and so it only flashed blue. He said he stood in the hallway as the police went in. He told Charlie of a system of flesh, like an engine of pink, a factory of pleasure. He told of the pale bodies of poor young women and the reddish bodies of men with bad tattoos—distorted cartoon characters mostly, sentimental yet sordid commemorations of the sanctuary of childhood that had stained their skin. The smell of the girls was like rotting flowers. There was a concentration of needle marks in the blond's right arm, and Whit figured she was left-handed. The brunette spat on the arresting officer's badge and told Whitaker that the "pig" was one of her best customers. As he went on and on, he wondered if Charlie knew he was lying. He wondered if Charlie would ever ask another renter about hearing anything.

"Well," Charlie said. "They probably had diseases anyway."

"Yes. Diseases."

"We all got some disease, eh, Whit?"

"Sure."

"Set me up for a wake-up call at 9:30."

"All right."

"Time to hit the hay."

Whit listened to Charlie's footfalls up the stairwell—slow, determined steps, like those of a prison guard. It didn't seem to matter to a guest if what Whit said was a lie or not, just as long as he told them something and made it real, just as long as he gave them another tale to tell along their routes. People loved to roll in each other's crap, like dogs. They reveled in stories of failed jobs, abusive childhoods, self-destructive tendencies, or sordid, distraught relationships.

Whit waited for the last of Charlie's steps. Then there was just the low hum of the fluorescent lights. He pushed himself away from his desk and went to wander the hallways. Before Albert, the daytime clerk, had gotten off his shift, he had told Whitaker about each person who had checked in. As Whitaker walked the halls, he tried to guess which guest was in which room: an old French woman dressed in yellow—yellow shoes, yellow dress, yellow umbrella—who had come from Leeville, Louisiana, to visit her grandchildren for the first time; a family of four, the two children with long, unwashed hair and no shoes; three Indian businessmen who had paid in ones and fives; an off-duty cop from Lake Charles who had come in with a stunningly beautiful young woman. There was no way to tell from the plastic number plates on the door, no way to tell from the locks, no way to tell even from the DO NOT DISTURB signs hung on a few knobs, who was in each room. There was no way to tell except by the feeling he got. And Whitaker had no feeling at all.

But when he came around the corner past the soft drink machines and saw the girl huddled in the hall, he knew she was the beautiful wife of the Lake Charles cop. She sat to the side of the corridor between room 158 and the door to the fire escape. Her ginger-colored hair was shoulder-length. Her face was thin. She had the lithe, worn body of a runner.

"Miss?" Whit said. "Are you all right?"

She looked up at him, and her hair fell across her mouth.

"Whitaker?"

"Violet."

Her left cheek was purple and raw, her eyes rimmed in red. Her irises shimmered like water in a copper bowl.

"What happened?"

She looked at her hand, the gold ring on her finger. "I heard you were working here," she said.

Whitaker took her to the general manager's office. He fetched her a motel towel full of ice, and as he held it over her eye her jaw began to quiver. "He's a policeman," she said.

"Who is he?"

"Evan Watts." She was quiet for a moment. "We got back together, then we got married at the J.O.P in Lake Charles. I don't know why. I should have known with his mustache. Only fascists wear mustaches these days."

"What happened?"

"He wanted to take me down to the strip club. I didn't want to go. So we fought."

"You've got to get away from him."

"Just stay with me a few minutes," Violet said. "Please."

"All right."

He stepped away from her and stood in the doorway.

She watched him with one eye, her head cocked back like the hammer of a pistol. "You lied to me, Whitaker."

He felt as though he might stagger and fall. "No. I didn't—" He was quiet a moment. "I'll just let you be. If you like I can call you a cab or—"

"I'm sorry, Whitaker. I don't mean anything. But why did you go?"

On the ceiling above, a palmetto bug crawled, as if moving across the top of the sky. "I was scared, I guess."

"Whitaker, will you just sit down and tell me about something, just anything?"

He closed the door and sat on a folding chair on the far side of the general manager's desk. He had sat here eight years ago, two weeks after high-school graduation to interview for his present job. He cleared his throat. He had a story, something he had planned to tell one of the handsome bastards over a martini.

"You remember the tiger? The one they kept in that cage at the gas station? Remember how they used to keep real tigers at those gas stations?"

"Yes."

"Do you know what happened to it?"

"He escaped or something."

"That's right. My first month working here."

"At the motel?"

"Yes. The hotel. I was with him when he died."

"You were?"

"Yes. One of the attendants at the gas station had taken his friends over to look at it one night. They were drunk. One of them pissed on him from the top of the cage. It turned out the cage wasn't locked properly, and the tiger ran. I was walking across the parking lot and heard someone yelling at me from a car. Mr. Stewart. He said he'd shot the tiger and he was going to get the owner. He told me to go over to the pasture beyond the fencerow of the cane field, the one just off the interstate. He gave me his rifle and a flashlight and told me to keep watch, but to not get too near the crazy son of a bitch. Crazy son of a bitch, he said. He said the tiger had killed a calf in his pasture. He was pretty sure the tiger was dead, but he wanted me to watch him until he came back with the owner."

Whit told her how the man had dropped him off at the fence and guided his flashlight to the place where he had shot the tiger. He held the flashlight on the animal, its black stripes curving like scimitars.

"I kept the light fixed on him. I couldn't seem to help it, but I climbed over the fence and walked toward the tiger. He lay on top of a calf with his legs collapsed under him. He'd been shot while feeding. As I got closer I could hear my heart, and I picked up some concrete rubble and threw it to see if he'd move, but he didn't. By then I was just a few feet away."

Whitaker looked at Violet. She held the towel in her lap. Her eyes were full of tears.

"His head, his face and jaw, was splattered with blood. The ground was splattered with it. Then for some reason I set the gun down and squatted, and his eyes turned toward me. I touched his head and his fur was sticky, like cotton candy. His eyes looked up at the stars. His chin was matted with blood, and it rested on the hindquarters of the calf. He'd been struck in the spine. Only his eyes moved. They kept looking from me to the sky.

"Then a car started down the service road, looking for a way into the field, but it missed the gate, and the taillights shrank away. A wind started across the cane fields, and it was then I felt heat coming up off the calf, even though it was dead. The tiger's tongue slipped from its mouth into the blood-soaked grass. I heard cattle off in the corner of the field. The herd was congregating, watching us.

"For the past few nights the sky had been dark and starless, but right then the clouds pulled back, and I could see this collision of stars across traces of dark purple. The tiger was watching the sky too, like maybe he was watching for his own shape to take form in some constellation. Then all at once I could feel his misery, his years of pacing the length of the cage, floating off of him up to the stars. When I rubbed under his chin his eyes closed, and that was all there was to him. I got up, walked back to the fence, and waited for the car."

Violet nodded. The towel dripped on the concrete floor. "You're lying," she said. "That's all you've learned how to do is lie."

"Do you want more ice?" he said. He stood and took her towel and walked the hallway to the ice machine.

When he came back she was gone. I should have let the tiger live, he thought. I should have told her the thing limped off into the woods and was still out there, roaming the Atchafalaya swamp.

Later, back at the desk, Whitaker watched Evan Watts come into the lobby, swaying alongside two salesmen in sport coats. They slapped one another's backs and laughed like old fraternity brothers.

Whitaker followed Evan to room 158 and stood outside the door listening. He heard Violet crying, then there was silence, then the complacent, lazy tang of cigarette smoke curling underneath the door. Whitaker walked back to his place at the desk to wait for morning.

At just past eight Violet and Evan Watts walked arm in arm down the hallway into the lobby. Whitaker nodded to Violet as she passed, but she looked away. Her make-up covered the bruise and a baseball cap was pulled down, shading her face.

When Evan and Violet were halfway across the parking lot, Whitaker followed them to the pancake house near the overpass. Hidden by the bushes outside the door, he watched them. Violet lit a cigarette and pulled her cap lower. Her husband kept his head bowed over his plate of eggs and sausage. They did not speak. Whitaker inched forward, slipping a little on the mulch.

For a moment he wished to be back in the hallways of the hotel, pacing past the doors but never entering the rooms, never intruding on the lives of those who were just passing through. He looked over his shoulder at the sun, which was now slicing its way above the pink hotel. He turned and stepped out from the bushes. Grabbing the door handle, he felt the sun press like a warm hand at the back of his neck.

Swimming in Hydrus 1997

THE FAMILY PONTOON BOAT WAS LIT WITH small candles on the prow. Russell took Doreen's hand and told her to close her eyes before he led her along the narrow pier. It was late in the evening on her forty-second birthday. When she opened her eyes, the boat looked like an enchanted ghost of the grimy boat she was used to seeing.

Russell had prepared sandwiches, submarined a twelve-pack of beer in the ice chest, and set out little white candles.

"I thought we could have an outing," Russell said. "Just you and me."

She looked back to the dark house to orient herself, then to the water once more. The dock lights of distant camps glowed along the twenty-mile crescent, a horizontal cluster of yellow stars, a constellation, around the shore. Doreen could remember learning in school the name of a star group that resembled the docklights. Going out to her parents' yard as a girl of fifteen, she would investigate the shimmering heavens. She could recall the shape of the constellation, but the name was gone from her. The water snake perhaps?

"What's all this?" she asked, looking down at the pleasant shadow-shrouded hull and the candlelight glinting off the lake's ripples.

"Happy birthday," Russell said. "It's for you. I wanted to do something for you. Whitaker suggested it. Something nice. But this is the only thing—"

She put her finger to his lips. "It's nice, Russell. It's very nice." She thought she might cry if he said any more. Russell clutched her, the delicate flames reflected in the lenses of his glasses.

As they cruised along the water, the breeze, a cool zephyr, calmed her more than the beer or the candlelight. Sometimes she peered over the gunwale where vague houses and gas stations and trailers tried to take shape, pale blue cutouts against the black night. The images came from the dark like ideas, unformed and fragmentary. Doreen closed her eyes to the reflections and listened to the motor churning the heavy water and frothing up a wake.

Russell stopped the boat in the center of the lake and sat down across from her. Occasionally another boat's lantern would hover along the distant shore, a passing bateaux accompanied by the high pitch of a whining motor. Doreen fancied the green lights as shooting stars trespassing among the fallen constellation.

"The reason I brought you out here," Russell said, "I mean besides your birthday is—"

"Russell?" Doreen looked at him, not as a wife who has lived with a husband for years, but as a young girl trying to listen to an excited boy.

"Yes?"

"Will you take off your glasses, please? There's not much light, and it ought not to bother you."

He looked as if it had never occurred to him that he *could* remove his glasses. She might as well have asked him to remove his head.

"All right," he said, pulling the glasses away and placing them in his breast pocket.

Doreen thought he looked terrified. "What is it, Russell? Is something wrong? Is it the boys? Is it Clayton?"

"No. He's all right. Whit's watching out for him. They went to Violet's apartment in New Orleans for the night."

"What then?"

"I wanted to tell you. I know I been a crap husband."

"Russell, you—"

"Doreen. No. Let me say this. I been working up to it. Now let me say."

"All right," she said.

"I know I been a crap husband. I could have been better. I been gone too much. I always mostly just did the wrong thing. Sometimes out of not seeing the truth and sometimes out of just wanting to do bad on purpose like."

"I don't know what you mean," she said, though he spoke the truth. Doreen felt like a dinner guest who won't admit the shrimp smells foul.

"You know damn well what I mean," Russell said. "You know, Doreen. Don't try to be nice about it. This is important to me."

"Okay," she said.

"If I had a choice I mostly chose wrong. And all I'm trying to say here is . . . you deserved better. I'm sorry. You deserved better when Ferdinand died and you deserved better when the boys were alone and when you were sick and when you weren't sick. You just plain deserve better. And I'm going to be that now. I'm going to. Because I love you, Doreen." There was more to the speech, Doreen knew, but he couldn't finish it then, not in the sentimental candlelight and not on her birthday.

When he began to cry, she pulled him to her, and they sat entwined without speaking for a long time. Two people, married for twenty-five years. Twenty-five years, she thought, and just talking now. What a waste. But she had known for a long time that she had stopped fighting with him and that she had shut herself off to him. It wasn't all Russell's fault.

"I want to have fun tonight," she whispered. "It is my birthday after all."

Russell sniffed and blew his nose in a handkerchief.

"Lets go swimming," Doreen said.

"We don't have any swimsuits," he said.

She shrugged, feeling a wonderful little buzz from the beer. She pulled her long patterned dress off over her head and felt the shock of being naked in front of him. She started trembling. Why? This was her husband. *Her husband.* But when was the last time he'd seen her naked? A year? Two years?

"You're the most beautiful woman I've ever known," he said.

She smiled, quickly mounting the helm rail and carving a swan dive of alabaster flesh against the night sky. Russell delivered a cannonball. They laughed and swam about, the lights bobbing on the horizon. She would enjoy the night. Though she had planned to tell him what the doctor had said, how it had come back, how it had been hiding deep within her and was growing again, she wouldn't tell Russell tonight. Tonight there were no doctors or children, no dead, no living, no houses, and no roads. There was only the water, fresh and black and joyful on her naked body, and a fallen constellation all around them, and a boy named Russell who'd been lost to her and was, for this moment, found.

Houston 1997

WHITAKER WALKED UP THE STREET to the drugstore on the bottom floor of the hospital. A pharmacist sat inside at the counter, staring at the green neon cross in the window. He was a skinny man with hairy hands and a nose like the beak of a snowy egret. He wore a white jacket, which, from the street, blended seamlessly into the Formica counter. Before him lay an open textbook.

Whit wanted to fill his mother's prescription before she woke up in pain again. The doctors had allowed her to stay with the family in a hotel room for Christmas Eve, so Whit had come over to Houston from New Orleans three days ago, leaving the shotgun house on Pearl Street that he was sharing now with Violet. The treatment center in Houston was the best in the region, and Texaco's insurance paid for the visits, and though the doctors said this was her final round of treatment, Whit hated to see her in pain. He hated too that, the day after Christmas, she would have to return to her small, dingy hospital room on the third floor.

He'd hurried past the chained doors of a church, the bolted glass doors of a shopping center, the restaurants and offices all closed and dark, before he saw the green cross glowing in the pane. The pharmacy window was like a pool of clear water in which the cross floated. All around Whit the city was dark and formless, buildings broken into mounds of brick, steel, and glass, and the mounds buried under the dark of a moonless morning.

Whitaker pulled at the door handle, but it didn't budge. The pharmacist turned from the cross and mouthed, "We're closed."

Whitaker looked at his watch. Just before five. He clasped his hands together, mock-pleading.

"All right," the pharmacist said. He went to the door and pressed a black button on the wall and the door cracked open. Cool air poured out to the street, and Whitaker suddenly realized how warm it was for December.

"What do you need?" the pharmacist said, lurching back behind the counter.

"Prescription. My mom is staying in the hospital, but they let her come and stay with us for Christmas. I need her pills."

"Oh?" the pharmacist said.

Whitaker handed over the prescription. "I don't know how to say it," he said.

"Yes. I have this in for—what's the name? Bush?"

"Yes. Bueche."

"Right. Bush."

The pharmacist ducked behind a partition of cubbyholes filled with pills. Whitaker waited. The medical textbook was open to a drawing of woman. Translucent skin below her breasts revealed her organs in green, yellow, and red. Her body was diagrammed and labeled with words that Whitaker did not know: *ampulla, fimbria, isthmus of fallopian tube.*

Whitaker surveyed the store. Baby formula filled one aisle, magazines with youthful faces glaring stupidly from the covers lined a rack. There were digestive aids, crutches, alloy canes on a shelf. A banner sagging from the ceiling read MERRY CHRISTMAS, HOUSTON!

The pharmacist returned shaking a plastic orange bottle, which he set on the counter beside the book.

"That'll be forty-seven fifty."

"Can you put it on her hospital card? She's still staying here."

"Sure."

The pharmacist began filling out a long form to credit the medicine. He wrote slowly and carefully. Whitaker hoped his mother wasn't awake yet. He began to fidget and make nervous small talk with the pharmacist.

"Do you get sick of being here?" he said. "On Christmas Eve and all?"

The pharmacist did not look up from his form. "I don't go in for Christmas."

"How's that?"

"Doesn't do anything for me."

"What's that cross in the window?"

"A pharmacy cross. It was here when I arrived. Be here long after I'm gone."

"Oh."

"I'm in medical school now. Going to be a doctor."

"No kidding." Whit shook his head. "I thought this was a religious pharmacy or something."

The pharmacist laughed. "No such thing. The only religion here is science. I guess you could say a pharmacist is the evolution of a priest. Christ, the churches don't even stay open the way we do. And if you ask me, science is truly devoted to human suffering, more so than religion."

The pharmacist had a perfect head of hair, as black as oil, and black plastic glasses. His left eye wandered as he spoke, and Whitaker could not be certain where the pharmacist was looking.

"It's sort of like this," the pharmacist said. "People come whisper strange Latin sounding words, pharmaceutical words to treat their sin. That's what we all have isn't it? Original sin, built right into the DNA? Sure. They come to me embarrassed about things in their blood, embarrassed about how they got it and just wanting to get rid of it. And that's the truth."

As much as Whitaker knew he needed the pharmacist's help he didn't want to be with him much longer. He wanted to go. If this was what knowing the truth did to you he'd take delusion.

The pharmacist dropped the bottle in a paper bag, which he stapled shut. "Here you go."

Whitaker hurried for the door, the pharmacist trailing him.

"Still warm out here?" the pharmacist said, stepping outside with Whit. "Doesn't feel much like Christmas, does it?"

"I guess not."

There was no sunlight yet, just a luminous haze over the city. The street was barren and expectant, its yellow lights blinking against the backdrop of glass buildings. Just beyond the pharmacy door the sidewalk had been torn away, exposing a dark, wet hole surrounded by three orange barrels and yellow tape.

"Some hole, isn't it?" the pharmacist said.

"What're they doing?"

"Water lines or something. Been like that for weeks."

They both stood perched at the edge, which disrupted the clean logic of the concrete, and peered into the hole. From a distance, Whitaker thought, they would look strange to someone walking down the street—a man in a clean white jacket and combed hair and a man in a black T–shirt and worn trousers.

"Sometimes I look up from the counter and there are people out here, businessmen, doctors, all types, looking down into it. It stops people for some reason. I think they stand here and think, 'This is where I'll be going, right into a hole.'" The pharmacist's left eye looked off down the street. His right eye gazed into the hole.

"Possible," Whit said.

They stood there for another moment as if waiting for something to emerge from the breach in the sidewalk.

"I better be going," Whit said. "My mom ought to have these first thing."

"Sure. Go on. Have a good Christmas."

"Thought you didn't go in for that."

"Have a good Christmas anyway," the pharmacist said, and he lurched back into the drugstore like a sentry returning to his post.

Whitaker walked back toward the hotel. He tried to keep up a quick pace, but he felt exhausted and anxious, and when he came to a brightly lit department store he stopped. A family of translucent plastic mannequins in Santa Claus hats stood in the window. A small slide projector on the floor projected photos of store items into each mannequin. The body of the father was filled with images of golf clubs, then the projector clicked and he was filled with polka dot ties, then wingtip shoes, then oxford shirts. The mother was filled with perfume bottles, scarves, gold watches, and shimmering diamond rings. The two child mannequins glowed with bicycles, tops, and baseball gloves.

Whitaker turned from the strange scene and looked at his hands. The body was a container that somehow held abstractions such as hate, love, and faith. But he knew these abstractions were dangerous, and they worked away inside of us like acid or flames. How much of life was feeling love and hate, despair and all the other abstractions burn inside of us and bring us pain? We could only take comfort that the love, the hatred, and the despair did not reside in us forever.

He had loved his mother and his father and his brother, and he still did. And he had hated them as well, hated himself at times too. His father had been filled with fear, his brother with madness, and his mother with love and faith and loss. They had all been strange and beautiful to him. And then there was Violet. She loved him now, and in her was his future, vast and unknowable. But all too soon they would recede and fade, their flesh no longer lit from within like fragile lanterns.

When he got to the hotel, the lobby was empty. He took the elevator to the seventh floor, and tiptoed into the room. A tall lamp shone a soft cone of light on his mother who dozed in a chair in the corner. A yellow and blue afghan was tucked under chin. She would get better. The doctors had said so.

On the twin bed near the door his father slept. His belly rose and fell as he snored. His glasses rested on the bedside table. Clayton sprawled on the floor, his hair disheveled, a comforter thrown over him. He looked like the little boy who had slept beside Whitaker all those years ago.

His mother's eyes fluttered open. He went and knelt beside her.

"Hello, Momma. How do you feel?"

"All right, baby."

She clutched a rope of cut-glass rosary beads, which a family friend had promised to bring back from a mission trip to Medjugorje. The friend had told her that the rosary beads had been prayed over by three priests at the site where the Virgin Mary was said to appear. But it wasn't so. The friend had called Whitaker and confessed that the beads she had promised had been lost with her luggage on the trip back home. The friend had bought the beads in a Christian gift shop in midcity Baton Rouge. Whitaker did not tell his mother any of this.

She was clutching the beads every time he came into the hospital room. Her fingers moved from one bead to the next even when she was in pain or doped up on medicine. The beads gave her strength, she said. If they gave her strength it didn't matter if they were real or not.

"What's it look like out there?" she said.

"Do you want me to take you to the balcony?"

"No. No. We'll wake your brother and father. Just tell me. Whisper it."

He said there was no one out. Empty buses rumbled down the boulevard. Birds chirped. Taxi cabs down on the boulevard made the sound of waves traveling up a beach. The western horizon was spangled with high-rise towers of glass.

"A city is man flexing his muscles at God," she said.

"In a way," he said. "I'm going to wash up. Take your medicine. It's time."

"Not just yet. I can't think straight on it. When you get out of the bathroom, I'll take it."

"You need to take it now."

She waved him off, and as the lamplight struck her scalp. He had gotten used to seeing the wig, the curly brown hair like a china doll's poking out from under her scarf, but she had taken it off to sleep. He saw now that there was still some life in her face.

"All right," he said, and he walked past the beds to the bathroom. On the hook on the bathroom door were the suits she had made him take care of. She'd made sure he had the suits cleaned and pressed. He got upset with her when she told him to do this, but she cried and told him it had to be done. It was the most important thing he could do to help her, she said, so he had done it.

At the bathroom sink Whitaker took off his shirt and washed his face. Looking in the mirror at his face and the hair on his chest, he felt old. For the first time in his life he didn't feel like a boy. There was a new feeling, like he had arrived at a different place and looked different from what he identified as himself. He thought about how many times he would change throughout his life. He would become different people at different times. A young man, a middle-aged man, an old man. But would he always be himself? What part of him would remain and what part of him would fade? For a moment he longed for boyhood, for youth, then he felt foolish for being vain.

He put on a clean button-down shirt and walked back into the room. His mother stood at the door to the balcony, one hand pressed to the glass, the beads dangling from her fingers. He walked over to her and touched the small of her back.

"You all right, Momma?"

She pointed to the pill bottle on the table, so Whitaker fetched a glass of water and the medicine, and she opened her mouth to him as if to take communion, and he set the pills on her tongue. He took the glass when she was finished.

"Open the door," she said. "I want to feel the air."

"Do you want me to wake Dad and Clayton?"

"Not just yet. They'll come too, soon. Help me up. I want to watch the sun come."

Lifting her was slow going, but soon they were standing. Her arms felt thin in his hands. She leaned on him as they slowly shuffled to the balcony.

He slid open the door and walked out into the blue light of the morning. There was no movement on the streets. She leaned on him and against the stucco banister.

Below, there were no voices. Only the rumble of vacant busses on the boulevard. Tiny chirps of birds rose from the U-shaped median. The sky above was still a darkened landscape. Slowly a white haze embraced the lowest quarter of the eastern sky. The horizon was spangled with dull blurry lights that rose in a geometric cluster of buildings, high rise towers of glass. When the low sunlight struck the dark windows, the panes turned aureate as rectangular golden pools.

"Everything will all right now, Momma."

"I know," she said, her face bowed in the warm clean light.

"Everything's behind us."

Whitaker didn't know what to say so he clasped her hands and was quiet, feeling there the familiar pattern of glass beads bound like a vine among her fingers.